About the
Red Fire

Book Four

The Real World Hero

E. L. Mendell

Book Four

About the Red Fire
Book four, The Real World Hero
By E. L. Mendell
Copyright ©2024
All rights reserved.

Printed in the United States of America. No part of this book may be used or reproduced in any manner whatsoever without written permission except in the case of brief quotations embodied in critical articles and reviews. All people and facts in this book are fictions. Any resemblance to real people or facts is coincidental.

Snow Dragon Publishing
Shelby, OH. 44875
First Printing 2024
Cover art by Abigail Mendell
Printed on acid-free paper

Library of Congress Control No: 2023948034
ISBN: 978-1-950218-04-2

Snow Dragon 2024

To My Friends, Dana and Saito
Thank you for your honesty when I
brought my book-related concerns to you.

Table of Contents

Book Four

Cast of Characters

Fasentario
(*fa-sen-tear-ee-oh*)

Fevros
(*fev-ross*)

Vilna
(*vil-nah*)

Etakai
(*eh-tah-ka-ee*)

Reitrin
(*ray-trin*)

Shan Kaffie
(*sh-ahn*) (*ka-fee*)

Clyde
(*k-lye-d*)

Xitou
(*zeet-ow*)

Hiro
(*hee-row*)

Aoiro
(*ah-oy-ee-row*)

Book Four

8

Chapter One
The Child in the Ocean

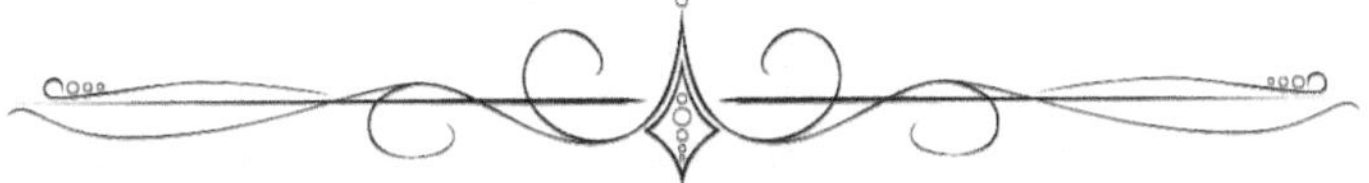

The ocean roared beneath the black sky of swirling storm clouds, lightning, and pounding rain. Waves tall as mountains thrashed the royal ship, *The Grand Inviolable*, as it fought the storm. The water crashed onto the deck and sailors shouted. They were tying down what had come loose and hanging on for dear life each time the ship heaved and tossed a new direction.

At the stern, Captain Fasentario stood his ground.

His feet were planted, his knuckles were white, and his green eyes were stony with concentration. He had fought storms like this before. The thick drops pelting his face and drenching his dark brown hair did not faze him. He kept the ship from capsizing as the water rushed aboard and rocked it like a child's toy.

"Starboard!" Fasentario called as a large wave approached.

The crew lunged to the starboard side. Their combined weight helped keep the ship from tipping when the wave crashed into it. They had sailed under the leadership of Fasentario for years. The captain was feared, yet held with the greatest respect.

Fasentario was commander of the royal fleet and had survived storms, pirate raids, and other nuisances on his journeys aboard *The Grand Inviolable*. He was always the first one the king requested when transportation was needed for trading, or to bring a royal envoy across the ocean.

Blinking rain from his lashes, Fasentario glared at the sky. The storm felt worse than any he had faced before. Perhaps because he was desperate to arrive home and not merely enduring the journey?

Fasentario gritted his teeth. His wife needed him. Her letter had been sent weeks ago and only reached him by luck. Fasentario had finished the details of the journey, which had been to personally deliver a gift of fine silks from the king to the foreign land, when a messenger brought him the letter.

He had read it then rushed the crew back to the ship. The crew was not happy about this. Fasentario customarily gave them a few days time to relax on land before they put to sea again, especially on long journeys like this. Not one of the crew readily accepted their Captain's decision.

The storm had been raging since before nightfall and made the mood of the ship match the sea's tempest.

On the horizon the clouds opened and Fasentario saw the sun shining through a red glow. He breathed a sigh of relief.

"Dawn has come," he called.

None of his crew cheered for the good news. Their silence and weary glares were unsettling. Fasentario frowned. He had anticipated their foul mood.

"Captain!" Fevros, the right-hand man of Fasentario, burst out of the cabin and slipped on the wet wood. He flailed his arms to stop his fall then spun around, looking up at Fasentario who grinned down at him.

"What?" he called.

"The storm is broken," Fevros pointed to the horizon and Fasentario chuckled.

They had navigated the storm and sailed on waves of manageable size. Fasentario loosened his grip and slouched forward to breathe.

Fevros hurried up to Fasentario, taking the steps two at a time. He wore the dark purple clothing of Ranoxto royal fleet and had badges on his chest, though not as many as Fasentario. The purple clashed with his lightning blue eyes but complemented his black hair.

"Well done, Captain," said Fevros, clapping him on his back.

Fasentario winced and shot him a glare.

"Sorry," Fevros looked embarrassed, but then whipped out the map. "Look," he exclaimed happily. "The storm blew us right back on track. We should be able to reach home in three weeks."

Fasentario took the compass and map from him to check for himself.

"Well, that's good to know," he said. His voice was calm and deep like the ocean and most people who met him were eased by it. "You are glad to be near home too, I take it?" He handed the compass and map back to Fevros, who was practically bouncing on his feet with excitement.

"I have my reasons," said Fevros, smirking at the captain.

"Secret reasons?" Fasentario cast him a wary look, but Fevros ignored it and his question.

"Why are you so anxious to go home? I've been meaning to ask you, but you looked too…" he hesitated when he saw Fasentario's expression melt to grief. "Sad." Fevros finished his sentence with a frown.

"For good reason," Fasentario sighed, looking up as one of his men climbed the ropes to the crow's nest with a telescope in hand. "I received some bad news while we were away."

"And?"

Fasentario ran his hand over his damp face and through his soaked and tangled hair.

"My son died."

Fevros froze. His excitement deflated. "I'm so sorry."

Fasentario shook his head. "He was born premature and too weak to fight off sickness." He gazed across the ocean. The storm clouds were passing over and sunlight touched the ship. "I need to be with my wife. I'm such a fool. I should never have left her alone with the infant when I knew he was ill."

"Occupational hazard," said Fevros. "A mission for the king can't be rejected, and you know that."

Fasentario did not reply. He had straightened up and was squinting to see into the distance.

"Lookout," he called to the crow's nest. The man above glanced at him and Fasentario pointed into the distance towards the sunrise. "Can you see that?"

The sailor held up the telescope and searched the ocean for what Fasentario saw.

"Man overboard," the lookout shouted. "Captain, it's a person!"

Fasentario left the wheel and leapt down the stairs onto the deck. "Lower a rowboat."

Fevros raced after Fasentario, rolling up the map as he went. "Captain, you should let one of the men go."

"No," Fasentario came to the boat as the men were lowering it. The ropes creaked on the damp pulleys as the boat came close to the water's surface. The waves were not yet calm and some were tall enough to lick the rowboat before it had reached the surface

"You're in an emotional state, sir," Fevros hissed to him so the men wouldn't overhear. "And after that storm the men will be agitated and angry. What if they …" he glanced around at the men lowering the boat. "What if they rebel?"

"Mutiny?" Fasentario glanced at him. "I know only one man here that would organize such a thing."

"Sir," Fevros tried once more, but Fasentario shook his head.

"I'm going, but I will return. Besides, you have things to tend to while I'm away, do you not?"

Fevros was glaring as the captain unrolled the rope ladder and climbed down to the boat. He took the oars and rowed away from the ship, leaving the others to watch as he shrank into the distance.

The waves rolled the small boat up and down as Fasentario drew nearer the drifter. The only sound was the plop of the oars dropping into the water and spray of droplets falling as they rose back out.

It was odd. There was no other rubble to suggest a ship had been bested by the storm.

Fasentario was unsettled by this.

The plank of dark wood was bobbing in the waves just ahead and now Fasentario could see someone lying on it in the fetal position.

Fasentario lifted the oars from the water and laid

them in the boat as it floated to the person. Fasentario reached out of the boat, grabbed the plank, and drew it close.

He thought his tired eyes were deceiving him. Lying on the wood was a small boy with silvery hair. He was wearing rags and was soaked. His nails were chipped from clinging to the wood and he was unconscious.

Fasentario took the boy under the arms and lifted him safely into the boat. The boy lay resting on his lap and Fasentario gazed down at him. The boy couldn't have been more than three years of age.

What was he doing in the middle of the ocean?

Fasentario pushed back the child's hair and discovered a fang tattoo under his left eye.

"Hello," said Fasentario, raising an eyebrow. "You're an interesting lad. A little young for tattoos, aren't you?"

The boy stirred, but did not wake. Fasentario sighed and carefully laid the boy on the bottom of the boat. He removed his jacket and draped it over the boy to keep him warm.

"You're not very lucky," said Fasentario, smiling sadly at the boy. "I have a tendency to draw trouble to myself. Can you believe that? I'm about to go back to my ship and you know what I'll find?"

The sleeping boy did not answer and Fasentario looked out at his ship. He admired its majesty from afar. *The Grand Inviolable*, his ship and second home. The sight of her on the ocean without him made his heart ache and a sigh escaped him.

"I'm about to go back and find a mutiny."

Fevros did not have a good poker face.

Fasentario had suspected him of organizing a mutiny since before they left the island. The only way he could have stopped it was by shooting a few of his crew, but Fasentario didn't want to risk dying at sea and leaving his wife alone.

He had chosen to leave the ship so Fevros could take over, and hopefully his life would be spared.

It was the lesser of two evils.

"One thing you learn from years on the sea," Fasentario muttered to the boy as he picked up the oars and began to paddle back to the ship. "When you have to rush men off land and back onto the sea, you're in for an unpleasant journey."

Chapter Two
Mutiny

Fasentario brought the boat alongside the ship and the rope ladder rolled down to meet them. He took a deep breath to steady his nerves before standing to disembark. He lifted the boy over his shoulder and scaled the ladder with one hand. When he reached the top the boy was pulled from his arms then he was seized and thrown to the deck. He felt his wrists bound behind his back and then someone grabbed his hair and forced back his head.

His men, the sailors he had considered family, stood around him, weapons in hand.

Since Fasentario had expected this, his expression remained neutral, even when a sword was pointed to his throat.

Fevros held the sword, a twisted grin on his face. "Welcome back, sir."

"Should I tell you that I'm not surprised?" Fasentario asked. "You are not a good liar, Fevros."

"I wasn't trying to fool you," Fevros replied, pulling a pipe from his coat pocket. "I had business to attend to on that island and you and your letter about that dead baby ruined everything." He emptied the contents of the pipe on Fasentario's head and the captain shook it off.

"I have obligations," Fasentario said. "You could have remained on the island if you'd only told me. I would have sent another crew back to fetch you."

"No, you don't understand," said Fevros as he

refilled the pipe. "My business cannot be complete without you."

"Me?"

Fevros nodded and struck a match on the bottom of his boot to light the pipe. He shook out the match and flicked it at Fasentario's face.

"You see," said Fevros, puffing on the pipe and smirking at Fasentario. "I had assassins there ready to kill you so I could take this ship."

Fasentario gawked at him.

Fevros snapped his fingers, pointing at his face. "There's the reaction I wanted." He laughed and sheathed his sword as if his mission had been accomplished. "How could you not realize I am an expert liar? I didn't have assassins on that island. The mutiny was my plan for this story."

"I'm so glad you're pleased," Fasentario growled. "What are you going to do with the boy?"

"The drowned rat you caught for me?" Fevros glanced at the boy who was lying at his feet. "I'll throw you both in the brig until we arrive in Ranoxto. I'll even give you water to keep you both alive, but only because he's important to the story."

"He's what?" Fasentario could not make sense of Fevros's words.

Fevros waved them away.

The men forced Fasentario to stand and shoved him towards the hatch that led below deck.

"I thought you wanted me dead," said Fasentario over his shoulder. "Why bring me to our homeland?"

"No good villain should be predictable." Fevros's grin seemed to say this had been his plan the whole time.

Fevros turned to the sailor who had picked up the boy. He stopped him and looked down at the boy as one would admire a piece of significant artwork. "I have high expectations for you, hero." He waved for the sailor to take the boy away and watched them go. Fevros heaved a sigh and nodded. "Things are working out nicely."

Down in the darkness of the brig time passed slowly. One day seemed to drag on for months. Fasentario could not see the boy in his arms, but he could hear him when he breathed, moved, and when he woke up.

The child sniffled and whined. His blubbering didn't get on Fasentario's nerves though. The man cradled the child, whispering to him, telling him about home and Vilna, Fasentario's wife, and their garden outside the house he had built for her. He spoke of every nice thing that the boy might find relaxing.

Days and nights passed, the sign of time shown only through a thin crack in the boards above their prison. Fasentario comforted the boy when the ship wagged back and forth, being thrown by the waves, and shared the scarce water they were brought once a day. Together they waited with no food and just enough water to survive.

The boy must have been starving, but even if he was, he did not say so.

Perhaps the child couldn't speak?

Fasentario tried to count the nights. A week and a half? Two weeks? He woke sometimes, unaware he had fallen asleep, and wondered if he had slept longer than a day.

Fasentario was having difficulty recalling how many days he counted when the door was unlocked and opened.

Daylight spilled into the room. Fasentario blinked through it with a scowl.

He shaded his eyes with his hand and watched the man who stood in the doorway, silhouetted by the light.

"I must admit, your determination to live is impressive," said Fevros. "I feel I should reward you for giving yourself and the child a will to survive, even though death is so much sweeter."

Fasentario made no reply.

"How about I let you go home?" Fevros motioned to the open space behind him. "But as punishment I'll make you take that boy."

"Punishment," Fasentario repeated.

"I'm taking your ship, and your crew, and everything on it," replied Fevros casually. "I think giving you a troublesome half-dead child is a nice addition to your pains."

Fasentario knew his mind was weak from lack of food and sleep. He knew something wasn't right about what Fevros was saying, but he couldn't think straight enough to figure it out. Was his life in danger? Would Fevros stab him in the back when he walked past him?

"You'll let me go home?" Fasentario asked.

"If you cross my path again, I'll kill you," Fevros said in reply. "For now, I'll show you mercy."

Fasentario looked down at the boy in his arms. The small child was fast asleep. He needed food, and Fasentario knew he wouldn't get any of that if he stayed in the brig.

"Very well," said Fasentario, looking up at Fevros. "I'll accept your offer."

Fevros grinned. "I hoped you would." He leaned back, looking out at the brightness behind him. Someone was calling down to him, but Fasentario couldn't hear the words.

"Good," Fevros shouted in reply. He then looked back at Fasentario. "We're approaching Ranoxto's port. I'll send someone down to get you when it's time to go." He left, letting the hatch slam shut.

The noise made the child wake up. He began to whimper and look around.

"Hush now, it's okay," whispered Fasentario, stroking the boy's soft hair. "Soon I will bring you home and you will have a chance to eat and drink. Just hang on a while longer."

The boy looked up at him and Fasentario blinked. He could see the child's eyes by a thread of light seeping in from behind the hatch. It must have been a trick of the darkness, but it seemed like the boy had different colored eyes. One was blue, and the other was green.

Fasentario placed a hand on the boy's forehead, tilting his head back to get a better look. "Were you born this way?" he wondered aloud.

He was startled when the boy nodded in reply.

Fasentario frowned thoughtfully. "Do you have a name?"

The boy hesitated, but then shook his head.

"Don't be sad," said Fasentario. "I'll just have to give you a name, that's all."

The boy's eyes lit up with surprise.

"You can inherit my name, since I'm going to be taking care of you," said Fasentario, tugging at a strand of the boy's hair playfully. A grin crossed his face. "My name is Etakai. Etakai Fasentario. So that will be your name too."

The boy stared at Fasentario with wide eyes. "E…Eta…kai?" His voice was small.

Fasentario grinned. "No one calls me by that name. Not unless I'm in serious trouble with Vilna. I am always Captain, Sir, or Fasentario to everyone, so from now on you'll be Etakai for me. Okay?"

A smile spread across the boy's face and tears of joy filled his eyes. He nodded and leaned up against Fasentario who wrapped his arms around him.

Chapter Three
The Life of the Captain

The kingdom was a few miles inland from the port town, so word of Fasentario's return would not spread fast. He had asked some men he knew at the port to send word to the kingdom about the mutiny, as well as a message that he would come soon in person to give his report. They had agreed to do so, and both made mention of the awful state he was in and agreed that he was in no shape to enter the king's court.

Fasentario was exhausted just thinking about speaking to the king. He was not a pleasant man. All Fasentario wanted was to go home.

Home was a small log house built in the middle of the forest. It was hidden away from both the kingdom and the port town, just as Fasentario had always wanted.

In his youth he had built the cabin himself and moved there with his wife. Since he was a sailor, his wife knew he would be gone on long journeys all the time. She said she was happy to wait for him in the home he had made with his own two hands.

"It's as if you're always there holding me," she had said, the sweet smile on her face making her brown eyes sparkle.

Fasentario sighed sadly. He stood at the edge of the large oak trees and gazed at his home.

There was a vegetable garden to the left of the house, surrounded by a white fence and standing in the midst of it was a scarecrow. A modest setting, but it was all they required to live happily.

It was growing late. They had arrived before sunset, but Fasentario was hesitant to approach the door even as the sunlight began to fade.

There came a tug on his hand and Fasentario looked down.

Etakai stared at the house.

Fasentario turned back to his home. He knew he shouldn't hesitate any longer, but his feet were rooted to the ground in fear.

Before heading for home he had stopped to get food and water for himself and Etakai, and also paused here and there along the way so the boy would not grow exhausted.

His excuses were reasonable, but the truth was Fasentario was worried.

What was his wife going to think?

The punishment Fevros had spoken of was starting to become clear.

"Okay, Etakai," said Fasentario, glancing down at the small boy beside him. "Let's introduce you to Vilna."

"Vilna," the little boy repeated.

Fasentario nodded, managing a weak grin. "Come on." He led Etakai by the hand to the house. He knocked on the door, taking a glance at the darkening sky to figure out if his wife would be awake or finishing her supper. He could have walked inside, but somehow he felt it better to have Vilna let him in.

Was this choice also created by his fear?

Before he could come up with a conclusion, the door flew open. A beautiful brunette looked out at him holding a long knife at her side.

The woman's expression had been dark, but it shifted to surprise at the same time Fasentario's did.

He stared at the knife, then up at his wife who stared at the small boy, then back at her husband.

"What are you doing with that?" they both asked at the same time, Fasentario pointing at the knife and Vilna pointing at Etakai.

Fasentario managed a laugh. "I found this boy in the ocean before my crew committed mutiny against me," he explained. He dragged Etakai in front of him and Vilna knelt to look at him.

"He has different colored eyes," said Vilna, setting down the knife. "Did that happen because of the ocean water?"

"Ocean water doesn't work like that," laughed Fasentario. "Apparently the boy was born this way."

"Really? Do you think he was?" Vilna tugged on Etakai's silver hair and grabbed his face, pulling on his cheeks and then looking close at the tattoo under his eye. "He's cute."

Fasentario's happiness died when he saw her curiosity melt to sorrow.

"Vilna ..." Fasentario began to say, but his wife shook her head and looked up at him.

"What awful tidings you bring home with you," she told him, tears filling her eyes. "A lost little boy, and also a mutiny on your ship? What more bad luck can we have?"

"I feared it would be worse if I tried to fight them. I was released at port after being starved during the journey." Fasentario gazed down at Etakai. "I was also given this boy to bring home as punishment."

"Punishment?" Vilna straightened up, watching Etakai, who was peeking past her into the home. "It is … it is quite heartless."

Tears filled her eyes and Fasentario stepped forward, pulling her into his arms. She seized him and sobbed into his shoulder.

Etakai looked up at them, confused.

It was a long while before Vilna regained control and looked down at Etakai. Her eyes were puffy and red from crying. "What … what is his name?"

"Etakai," said the child before Fasentario.

Vilna blinked in surprise and looked sharply at Fasentario who winced.

"You gave him your name?"

"I thought it would grant him a bright future," Fasentario replied sheepishly. "Don't be angry, please? I had not slept properly or eaten in days when I named him. He seems to like the name."

Vilna shook her head, but then set her face in his shoulder, made damp with her tears. "I don't mind. I'm just relieved you were permitted to live. They could have killed you. Then … then I would have had no one." She sniffed and her shoulders shook.

Fasentario held her tight and looked down at Etakai. "Can we keep him?"

Vilna nodded and a smile crossed Etakai's face. He clapped his hands and raced into the hut to look around.

As soon as he was gone, Fasentario kissed his wife's head. "I did not wish to cause you more pain."

Vilna shook her head again and said nothing. Fasentario squeezed her and led her inside.

The interior was plain, but warm. A small

kitchen sat in the center, the den was to the left, and a door on the right led to the bedroom. There was an attic, but it was narrow and rarely used.

"Will you be returning to the castle to announce your return?" Vilna asked.

"Because of the mutiny I must return whether I want to or not," Fasentario sighed.

"Losing a royal vessel could cost you your life, right?" Vilna whispered, wringing her hands. "Shouldn't you go at once?"

"The king will hear of the loss along with a message explaining my delay to report. He'll be angry, but won't be able to use my tardiness as an excuse. He knows I'm loyal to the crown, and losing me would injure the state of our naval forces."

"Just because you're fortunate enough to have a good reputation doesn't mean you should lean so heavily on it."

"We both know this is the first time I've been tardy." Fasentario looked at her. "I plan on taking Etakai with me when I go. The priest should meet him."

Vilna looked up at him with surprise. "You think he is …" She stopped and glanced at Etakai, who was watching them from under the kitchen table. He seemed to like it under the table, like a curious kitten would.

Vilna turned away and cupped her hands to her husband's ear. "You think the boy is demon possessed?"

Fasentario shrugged. "He was adrift in the middle of the ocean. There was no wreckage besides what he floated on. It is too peculiar. I think the priest could use his gift to tell me if he is a good or bad omen."

"And when will you go?"

Fasentario pulled Etakai out from under the table and the boy giggled as he struggled to break free.

"In the morning," Fasentario told Vilna as he carried the boy to the couch and playfully dropped him on the cushions.

Etakai laughed and Fasentario smiled.

Vilna watched them with concern.

Chapter Four
This is Etakai

The Kingdom of Ranoxto was not a large place. The castle was located at the end of a long, twisty road and sat at the edge of a cliff. The road was empty. Trees and bushes were scattered near it. Down the road from the castle was the village.

Plain houses lined the main road with many small roads weaving between them. The bazaar, where one could buy whatever they needed, was set at the foot of the castle.

Fasentario explained all of this to Etakai, pointing it out as they walked and entertaining him with stories of occurrences in the village.

People they passed gave him and Etakai odd looks and Fasentario wondered what kind of gossip would be spread before the day was out. He was well-known in Ranoxto. Many people knew of his family, and the unfortunate passing of his son.

Many of them would think Etakai was a desperate attempt to fill a void. A void that the child would never fill, though rumors cared not for the truth. There might have been a few people that thought it was nice of them to take in the child, but when word spread of Etakai's different colored eyes all kindness would vanish.

Ranoxto was a land of superstitious people. Anything that was different they deemed evil.

Despite these worries rolling through his mind, Fasentario maintained his composure.

As they entered the bazaar Fasentario was greeted by friends and acquaintances. He had been gone a long time and many wanted to offer their sympathy for his lost son. However, when they saw Etakai the sympathies vanished and were replaced with curiosity or confusion.

Fasentario did not make much progress at first as he was stopped and questioned about his journey and Etakai time and time again.

When they finally left the crowd, Etakai was holding his free hand over his ear.

"Those people are loud," Etakai said.

"That's rude," replied Fasentario. "It's not kind of you to talk about people behind their backs like that."

"Oh," Etakai murmured.

The castle stood before them and the large gate that encircled it was closed. A single soldier stood outside the gate, a sword in his belt and a spear at his side. The emblem on his brown cloak marked him as Captain of the Guard. Beneath the cloak he wore armor. His face was hidden by his cloak's hood.

Etakai examined the man curiously.

"Fasentario," said the Captain. "Have a good voyage?"

"No, I did not, Marcus," replied Fasentario. "Was my message from port not delivered?"

"Oh, it came, but you know I prefer to hear these things directly from you, as does the king." Marcus looked down at Etakai. "Word spread that you had a boy with you. He looks about as old as my own son."

"Is Clyde fairing well?" Fasentario asked. "I heard he had taken ill too."

Marcus sighed. "He is well now. I am sorry for your loss." He examined Etakai again. "A strange youngster he is. I have never seen eyes like that before."

"I think he's from another land," said Fasentario, smoothing Etakai's hair. "He remembers nothing and acts like he's new to the world."

"Are you bringing him to the priest?"

Fasentario nodded. "I want to know if he can tell me anything about the boy."

Marcus opened the gate and allowed Fasentario and Etakai to pass. "If things go well, the boy and Clyde should meet each other."

"We'll have to wait and see," said Fasentario.

Marcus nodded and then turned his back on the gate as Fasentario led Etakai up a winding path that split off into two directions. One led to the tall castle made of dark stone while the other trailed off to a large garden surrounded by a lush green hedge.

Within this garden stood the chapel, a round building with the front doors always open and a white fence surrounding it.

The priest was a strange man. It was said he could see into the souls of men and know if the near future would be bleak or bright for the individual. Gifts and abilities such as his were rare, but not unheard of. A faint trace of magic dwelt in the land, but it was not powerful, nor used for evil. Occasionally, a baby was born with magical abilities. Such infants were given special treatment. The priest had been one such child.

Fasentario glanced down at Etakai as they made their way towards the chapel. What would the priest say about the boy?

Inside, the chapel was dark and the sharp flowery scent of burning incense filled the stone chamber.

It was lined with nearly fifty pews facing toward a flat area where the altar stood. Behind the altar was a long wall covered in candles, a handful of which were burning. There was a large book lying open in the center of the altar. On either side of the altar there were candlesticks, but none of the candles there were lit. A purple cloth lay across the altar and a cross necklace hung in the center of the cloth, dangling beneath the book like a spider.

Only one man stood among the sloping pillars and rounded roof when Fasentario and Etakai entered. A stained glass window high above the wall of candles cast an odd web-like shadow on him. He stood opposite the altar, facing the stained glass with his arms folded behind his back.

The priest wore a sweeping black robe with a red shawl around his shoulders. His hair was blond and trimmed short, showing the rosary that hung around his neck.

Fasentario's steps slowed before he reached the altar. He felt Etakai's eyes shift to him, but he didn't move.

He was stopped by words he had once been told by the priest.

"When you step behind the altar, your days of plenty will end." The priest quoted the same lines that were rolling through Fasentario's head.

"I remember," Fasentario told him. "I won't approach the alter." He felt Etakai's small hand tighten over his fingers.

"It is not something you can control, Fasentario. It's something outside your control. It will happen, someday soon," his voice was smooth as butter. The priest turned, looking at Fasentario with a kind smile. His light blue eyes caught the candlelight and sparkled, but any kindness he wished to present with his smile was ruined by a dark cross that was painted on his forehead.

It was an eerie tribal cross that every priest in their land wore. The tattoo was rare and if anyone other than a priest dared to wear it then they were sentenced to death for blasphemy. Such was the way of sacred things in Ranoxto.

The priest examined the boy, the smile lingering on his face as his eyes sought out something more than the boy's appearance.

His smile faded. He locked his gaze on Fasentario. "What is the child's name?"

"Etakai," replied Fasentario, trying not to shy from the priest's gaze. The priest and his unpleasant oracles made him uncomfortable. "Etakai Fasentario."

The priest allowed his eyes to snap back to the boy. "Etakai, is it?" He placed his hands on the altar, leaning forward. He paused, then turned his head away, coughing a little, and winced. He then turned back and raised a hand, motioning for Etakai to approach the altar.

Etakai instead looked up at Fasentario. He was quivering, his eyes wide.

"The priest is harmless," whispered Fasentario, releasing Etakai's hand and propelling him forward. "Just stand across the altar from him."

Etakai nodded wordlessly and did as instructed. He stood before the altar that was almost over his head in height. The priest on the other side was tall enough to reach over it with ease.

The priest held out his hands, palms up. "Place your hands on mine, please."

Etakai glanced over his shoulder at Fasentario who nodded once. Trembling, Etakai held out his hands and placed them in the priest's. The man's hands were cold and a shiver went through Etakai. He didn't want to look at the priest so he instead watched the book lying in front of him.

The priest closed his eyes, placed his thumbs onto the back of Etakai's hands and concentrated.

They were motionless and behind them Fasentario watched. He was worried about what the priest might say about the boy.

The silence dragged on and all one could hear was the crackle of the candles and wind passing through the open door. Beyond that Fasentario vaguely heard the grass and plants rustling in the breeze. He attempted to listen to the sounds, wanting to block out the people before him, but the attempt failed when the priest cried out, released Etakai's hands and fell backwards.

Fasentario gave a start and ran behind the altar to the priest who writhed on the ground, holding his head and gasping as if he couldn't breathe.

"What's wrong?" Fasentario took the priest by the shoulders to stop his thrashing before he hurt himself. "Can you hear me?"

"It's wrong," hissed the priest. "Wrong. The balance of our world is off. The world is doomed to destruction. The wrong cannot be righted in this world. It cannot be fixed in this place. Someone from beyond must come and save us. Only one can restore what has been made wrong in this world!" The priest let out a cry of anguish before lying perfectly still.

Fasentario sat back on his heels, placing a hand to the priest's neck to check for a pulse. He waited, but there was nothing. Fasentario took his hand away.

What did the prophecy mean?

Fasentario passed a hand over his face, but then glanced back at Etakai. The boy stood beside the altar, his face was pale.

Fasentario held out his arm and the boy ran to him. Fasentario brought his arm around the boy's shoulders, drawing him down beside him.

"It's alright," he said quietly. "The priest has been ill for a long time." He did not add that Etakai's future must have scared the priest enough to finish off his weak heart.

"Am I a demon?"

Fasentario stared at Etakai. The boy was shaking as he stared at the priest.

"No," Fasentario replied.

Etakai looked at Fasentario, but then his gaze wandered back to the dead priest.

Fasentario heaved a sigh. "We need to alert the guards and repeat the prophecy to the king, as well as give him my report. Then we will go home."

Etakai let Fasentario carry him out of the chapel.

The walk up to the castle felt like an eternity. Some guards passed by and Fasentario called them over to tell them what had happened. They ran to the chapel, leaving Fasentario to report to the king.

Cobblestones wove their way to the tall walls of dark stone and tall iron gate. It wasn't a huge castle, but it was ancient and carefully tended. The gates were open and the soldiers on guard saluted to Fasentario and Etakai.

Fasentario nodded once to them and Etakai tilted his head at them.

"They're stiff like armor suits," Etakai said, looking back over Fasentario's shoulder. "Do you scare them?"

"I scare a few of the soldiers, yes," Fasentario replied.

The throne room doors were open. Inside nobles were mingling, discussing matters of trade and politics. In turn they began to notice Fasentario and stared at him and the child.

"Your Royal Highness," Fasentario bowed and addressed the king who stood in the mix.

The king did not blend in with the other nobles. He wore a robe of black and red with an extravagant golden crown on his head and his brown hair hung just above his shoulders. He looked upon Etakai with doubt in his dark gray eyes.

"Captain," he called, motioning Fasentario forward.

The people standing between them moved away so the two could pass through. The two men met in the middle of the room and shook hands.

"Your news of the mutiny is disappointing," the king said. His voice was deep and though he was shorter than Fasentario he emitted a strong presence. "The loss of *The Grand Inviolable* is tragic, but we're glad you survived." He eyed Etakai who stared at him. "Who is this?"

"I found him adrift in the ocean," Fasentario explained. "His name is Etakai."

"A replacement son?" The king looked at Fasentario who winced. No one had said it out loud until then. The king was a man who demanded respect, but he lacked tact and could be unnecessarily cruel.

"No one can replace my son," Fasentario replied. He couldn't suppress the cold edge in his tone. "I named him Etakai because I could not think straight while I was imprisoned on my own ship."

The king looked unconcerned. "Losing a royal ship would normally cost you your life."

"I know this, sir."

"And so you neglected to report to me straight away?"

"I am not one to run from you, sir. My right-hand man, Fevros, designed the mutiny. I've been punished plenty and hoped I could request I keep my life at least to make up for the wrongs done to me and the kingdom. But if you decide my life is not worth keeping, I can only ask you show mercy to my family in return for the years I have served you most faithfully and grant them life and means to live without me."

The king watched him. "I will not have you killed, Fasentario. You're a fine captain and knight. To lose you would be more devastating than the mutiny."

Fasentario bowed his head. He was overcome with relief and could have cried.

"He could have you dead?" Etakai looked

curiously at Fasentario, who was alarmed by the small voice speaking up.

"Don't speak before the king, Etakai," Fasentario whispered to him.

Etakai clapped his hands over his mouth and stared at the king.

"Teach him proper manners," the king said to Fasentario. The threat in his tone was obvious to all those around them.

"I have another matter to bring to your attention," said Fasentario, looking grim as he lifted his head. "I brought Etakai to the priest. He had a fit after viewing the child's future. He died–"

Fury came over the king. He glared at Fasentario with such menace Etakai wrapped his arms around Fasentario's neck as if hoping to protect him.

"I see." The king turned his back to Fasentario who held his breath.

The entire room was rigid with fear as they waited for the king to speak. If anyone made a sound they could be killed on the spot.

It was not beyond the king to kill without excuse. Fasentario remembered once when a messenger brought tidings of a trade route being lost. In his anger, the king had used his sword to remove the messenger's head before the court.

"Have you told others?" The king looked back at Fasentario.

"I sent two guards to attend to his body," Fasentario replied. "That is all."

"Good." The king turned away again. "You are excused. Go home and rest. I will send word when I have need of you. And one more thing." He looked back, but his gaze locked on Etakai. "Keep that demon child out of the castle from now on."

Fasentario recoiled. He didn't have time to stop Etakai from hearing the words and the child stared at the king with alarm.

"Thank you for your time, Your Royal Highness." Fasentario bowed then hurried out of the throne room. He was practically running. Etakai still had his arms wrapped around his neck and he stared behind them until they were outside the castle.

"He said I'm a–"

"He may be the king but that doesn't mean he always speaks truth," Fasentario interrupted as they passed out through the gate. Marcus watched them go without a word.

Etakai had tears in his eyes. "But I'm not–"

"You're not a demon, Etakai," Fasentario stopped and looked down at him sternly. "You're my son now. I would not have accepted you if I sensed you were a demon. You were born far away. For all I know your uncommon appearance is common in another land. Do you understand me?"

Etakai stared at him.

Fasentario headed up the street. He took the long way around, passing outside the busy portions of the village. He didn't want to talk to others. His mind was racing and his blood boiled.

The king was out of line, but if he had said anything he and Etakai could have been killed.

It was dusk before they arrived home and Vilna met them outside. Fasentario told her all that had happened as he brought Etakai inside and laid him on the couch.

Vilna was frightened by the sudden death of the priest as well as the king's hostility.

"I will still raise little Etakai regardless of today," Fasentario told Vilna as they sat across the table from each other. "That is, if you approve this adoption?" He watched his wife, who was gazing at the table.

"Etakai," she whispered to her husband. "You have always had such a big heart, but this," she gazed past Fasentario to the couch where the boy slept. "I … I'm scared."

"Times are hard," Fasentario told her. "For a boy like him, his best chance would be to join our family. We can't let a few bad omens scare us away from doing what we know is right."

Vilna wrung her fingers, but then reached out and grabbed her husband's hands.

"I love you," she said, gazing into his eyes. "And you have not steered us wrong yet. So, I'll trust you."

"Thank you," said Fasentario gently.

From that day on they took care of Etakai. The boy was fond of Fasentario and would imitate him whenever he could.

Each evening when Fasentario came home he would take Etakai outside and teach him to fence. The boy was scared of their wooden swords hitting each other, and he flinched often.

"Keep your eyes on your enemy," Fasentario told him, slowly swinging the sword back and forth for the boy to block.

Though the boy did not enjoy swords, he was not defenseless. Vilna reported to Fasentario that she had seen Etakai throwing the kitchen knives outside. He hit the same narrow tree every time.

"His aim was flawless," Vilna whispered as Fasentario tucked Etakai in for the night.

"Small knives are easy," Etakai told his parents with a yawn. He rolled over and fell asleep.

Fasentario grinned and looked at his wife. Vilna smiled and took his hand. It was the first time she had looked happy since Fasentario brought Etakai home.

Time sped by and their lives were uneventful. For three years they lived peacefully. Fasentario did not go on long trips but worked as an advisor for the royal navy to remain close for his family. Losing a child while away haunted him and he refused any requests that came for him to set off across the ocean.

Etakai went out sometimes to meet Clyde, the son of Marcus, as well. They had become fast friends, as Clyde was too young to show prejudice against Etakai's appearance.

Fasentario was relieved to see Etakai make friends, but as time dragged on he began to feel uneasy.

He heard exaggerated rumors in the kingdom about bad fortune befalling everyone. They whispered of a bad omen and more than once a day Fasentario would see people cast him wary glances. It was then Fasentario knew he and his family were not safe.

It was not long after tongues began to wag that Fasentario came home in a dark mood. Etakai ran out to meet him carrying their wooden swords. Fasentario just ruffled his hair and went straight inside, calling to Vilna.

"I have bad news," said Fasentario when Vilna came into the kitchen.

Fasentario tossed down a letter with a red wax

seal. "The king," he said, his voice hoarse as he spoke. "The king …"

"What's happening?" Vilna whispered.

Fasentario cursed out loud and slammed his fist on the counter. He was pale. His knuckles were white. Vilna had never seen him like this before.

Etakai came into the house, putting aside the swords and watching his parents.

"I was brought that letter today," said Fasentario, dropping into the chair.

Vilna took it and read it carefully. Her eyes grew wide. "But this …" She gasped and looked first at Etakai, then to her husband. "This is nonsense."

"Nonsense or not," said Fasentario, rubbing his face as he spoke. "They want to take him away."

"Is this because of his eyes?"

"His eyes, his hair, his sudden appearance and lack of a past. I don't know who has been spreading rumors about him these past three years, but we can't let them take him on such biased accusations."

"Didn't you mention a few weeks ago that your old ship had been spotted not far from here?"

"Yes," Fasentario sounded grim. "I suspected Fevros somehow started the rumors. I don't know how he could travel in this land and avoid being arrested for mutiny. That man is clever, so even if I don't understand how it could be possible, I can't doubt that it is."

"Why would he spread rumors like this? It makes no sense."

"Back then he wanted me dead. I didn't understand why he let me go home with Etakai, but it seems this might be part of that reason. I'm so sorry,

Vilna. I didn't even think he would bring his wrath onto my whole family. After these three years I hoped his threat had faded."

"Fa?"

Vilna and Fasentario looked at Etakai who stood alone in the doorway. His eyes were filled with tears.

"Am I hurting you two?" Etakai sniffed, trying to fight back the tears.

Vilna hurried to him and pulled him into her arms. "No, that's not it at all."

"I won't lose another son," muttered Fasentario as he stood up and took the letter off the table. "We should leave."

"But you're a captain in the king's navy." Vilna was pale now. "They'd call it treason and kill us all. Your reputation won't be enough to stop it this time."

"At this point they're going to do that anyway." Fasentario crumpled the letter and threw it into the fire under the stove. "We have to pack tonight and I will figure out where we can go. We'll go through Burch Wood and once we get past the border, we should be able to start a new life. The king cannot send his soldiers after us if we disappear outside his jurisdiction."

Vilna looked down at Etakai, who was watching them with scared eyes.

"That isn't the life we wanted," Vilna whispered to her husband.

Fasentario gazed into the fire, but then looked at her and Etakai. "I know, but this is what we've come to. We need to escape alive and find a new life, for us and for Etakai."

Vilna bowed her head and held Etakai tight. The

boy gripped her arm.

None of them slept that night.

Vilna was packing and Etakai sat in front of the door waiting for it to open. Fasentario was outside keeping watch. He had armed himself with a bow, arrows, and his sword. Etakai had never seen him look so intimidating before.

Etakai looked over his shoulder to Vilna. She was crying as she folded clothes and tucked them inside a burlap sack.

"Ma?" he whispered.

Vilna shook her head, sniffing as she tried to keep back tears. "Your father is a brave man. He's defying the king's order to keep you and me safe."

Etakai looked back at the door. "I hear movement outside."

Vilna lifted her head and listened too. It was long past sunset and there were crickets outside. But Etakai was right, there was movement in the forest and it did not sound like the normal wildlife passing through.

Etakai stood up. "I'm going to check on Fa–"

"No!" Vilna grabbed Etakai's arm and pulled him back. "Stay here. I'll go find him."

"But I'm a soldier like Fa," Etakai cried, staring up at Vilna angrily. "Clyde and Fa both say so. I will go help him."

"No, no, you must stay here, please," said Vilna, holding his head in her hands. "I'll go after him. I'd feel much better knowing you're here and safe. Please stay here." She kissed his forehead then moved to the door, but Etakai ran after her, grabbing her hand to stop her. Vilna turned, and dropped to her knees, pulling Etakai into a hug and holding him tight.

"Be brave, Etakai," she whispered to him.

Etakai blinked, but then Vilna released him and went outside.

The door shut.

Silence filled the room.

Etakai stood by the door, gripping the bottom of his shirt in his hands and chewing on his lip. He watched the door listening to the sound of shuffling feet outside.

What if they didn't come back?

Standing there did nothing for his patience. He began to pace, watching the door each time he passed it, then looking at the ground.

A scream cut through the silence.

Etakai spun to face the door.

Everything went cold. He heard shouting. Raised voices were coming closer and Etakai took a step back. What was happening? He could hear a woman's voice pleading for help, but there didn't seem to be any. Etakai's heart iced over in fear when he realized the voice belonged to Ma.

And then her voice cut off.

Etakai ran to the door, but before he could grab the handle it flew open and slammed into him. Etakai was knocked to the floor, gripping his arm as it began to throb. He glared at the soldiers who stood before him, both of them wearing dark hooded cloaks that hid their faces.

"There he is," one laughed, walking into the house. "Right out in the open. I didn't expect that from Fasentario." He grabbed Etakai's arm, dragging him to his feet. Etakai kicked at the man, pulling as hard as he could to break free, but he was still only a child. The soldier's grip didn't loosen, not even when Etakai bit his hand. All that earned him was a slap across the face before they dragged him outside.

The night was red from the flames beginning to eat the hut. The scent of smoke filled Etakai's nose and he coughed, placing his free hand over his nose. The yard was filled with soldiers wielding swords and torches.

Two of them held Fasentario who stood with blood dripping from his lips. His dark hair was matted with blood and a bruise was forming over his right eye. He was unable to lift his head.

Etakai noticed Fasentario was staring at something that lay near the trees. Motionless. Etakai followed his gaze.

A shout of horror escaped him.

"Ma!" he screamed. He threw off the soldier's grip with unforeseen strength and ran towards the crumpled form of Vilna.

Three men tackled him, but Etakai squirmed out of their grasp, his terror blinding him of whatever pain he might be causing them or himself.

He raced to Vilna, grabbed her, and rolled her over onto her back. Her eyes were open, but they stared at nothing. There had been tears, but they were no longer falling. Etakai touched her neck, as he had seen Fasentario do to the priest, but the pulse was gone.

Then he saw the arrow that stuck from her ribs.

Rage surged through Etakai, bringing a fresh batch of tears to his eyes. He lowered his mother to the ground and closed her eyes. Then, with fists clenched and his gritted teeth bared, he stood.

He could feel the soldiers watching him. He knew they would shoot him down if he tried to run. Etakai slowly turned his head and looked at Fasentario.

A pit of fear sank into his gut when he saw an arrow sticking out of his father's stomach.

Etakai lifted his gaze to his father's eyes, and Fasentario gazed back. Etakai could see death was not far.

"What am I to do?" Etakai whispered.

The soldiers laughed at him. Whether for his tears or his weak voice, Etakai was unsure.

Fasentario saw the soft glow that had taken form in Etakai's green eye.

"I …" Fasentario winced, wheezing in pain. He tightly shut his eyes. "I want you to live. Please … live."

Fasentario released his final breath, and the guards dropped him. He crashed to the ground and did not move again.

Etakai straightened up and some of the soldiers laughed at him.

"What are you going to do now, squirt?" One mocked. "Run away and die like your mommy and daddy?"

Other soldiers joined in the laughter and Etakai lifted his head. The tears rolled freely down his face.

"No," he hissed icily.

One of the soldiers reached for him, but in a flash of green light the soldier screamed a blood-chilling cry. He fell to the ground, holding his arm that was burned raw up to his elbow. He stared at the child who glared at him. Green fire trickled from Etakai's eye like tears.

"Monster," the man whispered. He struggled to run away, hugging his burned arm to his body.

Etakai lifted his sight, his aura more menacing than anything the soldiers had faced before. The air itself told them there was no chance of escape.

"You wanted a demon, right?" Etakai's green eye blazed so bright that it illuminated the whole clearing. The fire on his home and each torch turned green and took on a new life. They cut spiral burns into tree trunks and the soldiers drew away nervously.

"Shoot him!" their leader barked.

Arrows flew at Etakai, but he flicked his hand, and the fire sliced the arrows away. They fell in pieces at his feet.

"I. Will. Never. Forgive. You." Etakai screamed at the top of his lungs. He lifted his hand and slammed it into the ground.

The forest floor erupted with green fire and the soldiers screamed.

Etakai clenched his teeth. He heard the burning soldiers running for their lives. They tripped over each other to escape. One by one, they collapsed between the trees, unable to beat out the green flames that ate them whole.

Dizziness overtook Etakai and he raised his hand from the ground. He gasped for air, closing his eyes. When he opened his eyes again, his sight was fading in and out.

Etakai looked around the burning woods. There were dead soldiers everywhere. The stench of burned flesh mingled with the smoke that hung in the air. It made Etakai gag and he hunched his shoulders, covering his mouth. He pushed himself to his feet and staggered to Fasentario. He collapsed beside him and touched his father's face.

"Fa," Etakai's lips trembled. He leaned forward, sobbing into his father's back until the dizziness overtook him and he passed out.

Chapter Five
Waking Up

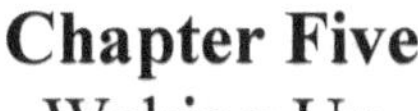

"Be brave, Etakai ..."
"I want you to live. Please ... live..."

Etakai slowly opened his eyes. The gray light around him told him it was morning. He blinked, then sat up. He had been asleep on Fasentario's back. Etakai rubbed the dry tears out of his eyes.

The forest was replaced by burned trees and ashes. The sunlight was cloudy and gray within the destruction. The fire left a path of destruction as far as Etakai could see. Ash fell from the sky when the wind blew. It spun on the updraft and some brushed against Etakai, leaving remnants as they passed.

Etakai wiped the ashes out of his hair. He looked around at the dead soldiers. They were nothing more than charred corpses. Etakai turned to the hut, but it had been burned down also.

Nothing remained.

Etakai knew he should run away before more soldiers came. Vilna and Fasentario had died in hopes of saving him, but he couldn't leave them where they were. He stood up and went to Vilna. Taking her under her arms, he dragged her to Fasentario's side. It was difficult, but when they were beside each other he stood back, and nodded once in satisfaction.

It now looked like the two of them were just sleeping side-by-side. They would have wanted to be together in the end.

Etakai forced back tears and turned away,

walking into the forest alone. He would look for Burch Wood, since that was where his father planned to go. From there he would find a way to live his life. How? He wasn't sure. There were no answers for his young mind. Would he starve to death before he found a place to stay? All he knew were ways to defend himself and a little reading and writing.

Neither of his parents had known he would have to fend for himself. He needed help. But who would help a demon?

Etakai had to suppress more tears. His odd eyes had brought misfortune to his parents. They had risked their lives to take him in, and in the end, he was the reason they were killed.

"Live," Etakai whispered to himself, wiping his eyes dry from the threatening tears. "Fa said to live."

For a long time, he walked through ashes and burned forest. He kicked up a trail in the dust and watched the ground as he went.

The green fire had done a lot of damage.

"What was that power?" Etakai asked, reaching up and placing his hand over his green eye. "I wish I knew how I did that."

A bird sang from the trees; the first sound of wildlife since he started his journey.

For hours he was surrounded by gray and white ashes and broken trees. He climbed over fallen trunks, ducked under half-fallen trees, and slid down slopes. The further he went the more he began to notice green grass beneath the ashes. Soon he was surrounded by trees that bore no damage.

Etakai stopped and lifted his head to look around. He was now in a new part of the forest. He wondered if it was Burch Wood.

The trees were much larger and looked ancient and the only ashes were those that the wind had carried over. It was nice to see the green grass again. Etakai sighed and continued to walk, though now he kept his head up.

Night fell and still Etakai walked. The thought of food didn't cross his mind. All he could think of was the soldiers attacking. He wondered if there was a way to obtain revenge. They had hurt his family, and now he wanted to hurt the ones responsible for what happened. Like the king, who had caused all of this. Was there a way he could? He was magical, though he didn't know how to use it. Maybe he could avenge–

Etakai tripped and tumbled down a slope he hadn't seen.

He fell head over heels through the tall grass, struck the ground on his back and lay motionless for a long while. He stared sourly at the dark sky that was slowly turning pink, signaling the approach of morning. Had he walked all night?

Etakai made a mental note not to think so hard while walking. He didn't want to end up making a fool of himself, as he had just done.

"At least no one saw that," he muttered to himself as he rolled to his stomach and pushed up to his knees.

He rubbed his silvery hair, but then blinked when he saw two feet standing a little way ahead of him.

His head shot up and he stared in alarm at the girl who stood there.

She held a basket in her hands that was filled

with mushrooms and covered with a towel. Her gray dress had dirt around the hem. She was skinny and her brown hair was tied back in a high ponytail.

Her mouth hung open, and she lowered her basket, staring at Etakai.

"Where did you come from?" she asked, her green eyes traveling up the trail of smashed grass he had left. "Did you fall from the sky?"

Etakai pouted. "No, just higher ground." He stood up and dusted himself off.

The girl was still staring at him and Etakai sneered. "What? You never see a demon before?"

The girl tilted her head. "Is that what you are? I thought you were just a special looking boy with a torn shirt."

Etakai looked down at himself. His shirt really was torn. He placed his hand over it, blushing.

Did the girl know who he was? It was possible he had traveled so far that he was no longer within the land of Ranoxto.

Had the stories of Fasentario's demon boy traveled to this girl's home?

"Who are you?" the girl asked. "I heard there was a fire in the woods last night. I'm surprised to see a child like you wandering around out here. Where are your parents?"

Etakai glared. She was a child too. How dare she speak to him like that? She wouldn't dare if she knew what a monster he was. "My parents died in the fire."

The girl gasped and dropped her basket of mushrooms.

Etakai looked away from her. "Now I have to find a place to stay. Fa told me to live. I don't know how I will do that though.”

"You can stay with me and my father," said the girl. "I am sure he won't mind."

Etakai was surprised. "I told you I was a demon. You shouldn't show kindness to me."

The girl giggled. "If you're a demon then I'm a pond scum creature from the depths of Orani Marsh. What's your name?"

"Uh …" Etakai hesitated. He didn't want anyone to know his last name. Fasentario had enemies, and Etakai didn't want to bring trouble to this girl.

"Etakai," he said. "Just Etakai."

The girl giggled again. "That's a funny name. I'm Alia." She held out her hand in greeting.

Etakai hesitated, but then slowly reached out and shook it once.

"Come on, now," she said as she gathered up her basket and scooped the fallen mushrooms back into it. She grabbed Etakai's arm and dragged him off into the forest. "I'll show you my house and introduce you to my father."

Etakai stared at the back of her head, but then a sad smile touched his face. Maybe it would be safe with Alia. She didn't judge him like the other people had and she didn't think he was a demon.

*   *   *

Twelve years passed.

Night fell in Burch Wood. Tree branches creaked and leaves rustled. In the distance tree frogs sang.

The long road that reached outside the borders of Ranoxto was empty. On one side of it was the forest, on the other side were long fields of corn and wheat stretching as far as the eye could see. A single

53

farmhouse peeked out of the field in the darkness, but beyond that were only trees covering the horizon.

From up the road, the clip-clop of a horse's hooves and the squeaking of a wagon cut through the night. It made its way up the curving road and towards the designated area.

The carriage stopped at the bend. The horse tossed its head, pawing the ground and snorting as the driver climbed off the carriage and went to the back.

The driver wore a long robe with the hood pulled up and a rope tied around his waist. He examined his surroundings before opening the back of the carriage and crawling inside. He emerged with a crate in his hands. His eyes scanned the surroundings once more before he whistled and threw the crate into the darkness of the woods.

Someone caught it, tossed it to another person hidden further off, and then it was tossed again to another, and on and on until it was out of sight.

The man crawled back inside and withdrew another crate. He tossed it to the woods like before. As the next crate was being tossed down the long line of hidden people, someone left the shadows and stepped out into the road near the horse.

He glanced around before following the man's tracks to the back of the carriage.

"Any followers?" he asked. His blue eye was glowing softly so he could see through the night to the man who tossed another crate into the woods.

"None this time, Etakai," replied the man in a lowered voice. "The soldiers thought it was suspicious that I needed so much from the market. I told them some story about me having a vision of a famine. The fools bought it, but we'll have to be careful next time."

Etakai nodded once and watched as Alia's father tossed the next crate into the woods. He knew that at the end of the line was another carriage that would take the supplies to their hide out.

"Oh," said the man, climbing out of the carriage with another crate. "I'm supposed to tell you that Alia sends her greetings."

He then tossed the next crate. It was second nature to all the men to catch and throw the crates through the darkness. This way they would not form paths to their hiding place. Secrecy was safety.

"Is she doing well working at the school?" Etakai asked, watching Alia's father as he took the next crate and tossed it.

He paused this time after Etakai's question and sighed. "She's been taken as a tutor for the prince." His wrinkled face showed beneath his hood and Etakai saw the worry in his eyes. "I was only allowed to see her for an hour before they chased me away."

"Will she remain in the school?" Etakai inquired. He kept the fear for his childhood friend out of his tone.

"No," said the man angrily, crawling into the carriage again. He came back with another crate that he glared at momentarily before chucking into the woods.

"Gah!" someone shouted from the darkness.

"Be careful," Etakai sighed. "The crates and the men need to remain intact."

"They're keeping her inside the castle, Etakai," Alia's father growled. "It's as if someone wants to use her as bait to get to you. There's no other reason for placing a tutor inside the castle. She should be left in the school house. It bothers me."

"We can't have that," Etakai muttered. "I'll go and check on her."

"For you to go see her is exactly what they want."

"I've been in and out of the castle before," Etakai said. "It'll be fine."

The man only grunted in reply as he cleared out the rest of the carriage. Etakai stood by, passing his hand over the belt of throwing knives he wore around his waist. He checked the sky, estimating how late it would be if he traveled to Ranoxto by foot.

"If I leave now, I'll be there by tomorrow evening," said Etakai. "It should work fine."

Alia's father sighed as he tossed the last crate into the woods. "If you bring misfortune on her I'll kick you out of the rebellion," he said under his breath, closing the back of the carriage.

Etakai knew it was a joke, but he didn't laugh. "You can't kick me out. I started this rebellion."

Alia's father shrugged. "Then you can kick me out." He walked past Etakai to the front of the carriage.

"If I have to, I'll take her out of the castle and bring her to the hideout," Etakai sighed.

"You may have to do that," sighed the man, climbing up onto the carriage and taking the reins.

"What do you mean?" Etakai asked. He had wanted to keep Alia away from the rebellion. Letting her stay safe in Ranoxto working as a teacher had been the best way to ensure she wouldn't be caught in anything dangerous.

"I want her safe, Etakai," said Alia's father. "People are beginning to suspect she knows you."

Etakai felt worry grip him. "I'll look into that while I'm there. I give you my word, she will be safe."

Alia's father shrugged and snapped the reins.

Etakai watched him go, his gaze traveling further up the road.

He had not visited the kingdom in a long time. When they were children he and Alia would accompany her father to market. Now that he was grown, Etakai couldn't risk walking into the kingdom during the daytime.

Etakai stepped into the shadows and began the long walk to the kingdom.

As expected, he arrived after sundown.

He had made the journey plenty of times in the last few years in his life, but this was the first time going to infiltrate the castle for reasons other than collecting information.

Etakai slipped past the night guards and crawled along the stone walls to the back of the castle. He searched the windows, moving slowly and quietly. If he were caught the soldiers would try to kill him. It was not hard for anyone in Ranoxto to recognize the demon son of Fasentario, even now that he was full grown.

Alia's window was ajar so the night air, and maybe stealthy enemies, could get in.

Etakai shook his head. He wished Alia would be more careful. Had she not anticipated someone dangerous could come in? She still thought and acted like a child sometimes, even after Etakai and her father explained she could be put in danger at any moment.

Did she think the castle was safe?

Etakai pushed open the window to look inside.

The room was quaint, round, and had a red and orange rug in the middle of the stone floor. On the bed sat Alia.

Her brown hair was tied up with a ribbon. It was sloppy, as if her only goal had been to keep her hair out of her eyes. Her head was resting on her hand. She wore a nightgown with a brown bathrobe over top and her feet were bare. Settled on her crossed legs she held a book with one hand holding the pages. She turned the page and continued to read without noticing the man in the open window.

Etakai slipped into the room and watched her for a moment to admire her.

"Knock, knock," he said.

Alia leapt from the bed and hurled the book at him.

Etakai caught it with one hand and flipped it over to peer at the pages.

"What. Are. You. Doing. Here?" Alia hissed, wrapping her robe around herself tighter.

"You're coming with me," said Etakai, shutting the book and dropping it on the bed.

"Why?" Alia demanded. "I thought I could collect information here."

Etakai held her gaze. "It isn't safe here. People have begun to suspect that you're connected to me. You'll have the entire royal guard outside your door if they decide to act on the rumor."

"Etakai," Alia said softly, but then she looked away. "I didn't know that. I just wanted to be of some help to you."

"You should be smart enough by now to know you're in danger within these walls," Etakai retorted, his voice icy. "I can't protect you if you're here."

Alia rubbed her arms, watching the floor sadly. "I'm sorry,"

Etakai sighed. "You can't stay here. Your father wants me to take you with me. My men will have a fit about a girl being in the hideout, and you might not enjoy it much either, but you've left us no choice."

"I lived with you and Pa," said Alia in defense. "I know very well what men can be like."

Etakai rolled his eyes. "That's not the same, but it doesn't matter. Pack up your things."

"Ah! H – Hang on," said Alia quickly. She hurried through the room, moving things here and there and shoving her personal items into a shabby bag.

As she packed, Etakai listened for guards outside the window. He had a bad feeling and lifted his head just when there was a knock on the door.

Alia froze and stared at Etakai who motioned for her to answer.

"Who is it?" Alia called, creeping towards her bed and hugging her bag to her chest.

"Who else would it be?" the man on the other side asked. "I still have questions for you, Alia."

Etakai uttered a curse and glared daggers at Alia who hunched her shoulders. He knew who the man was. The fact Alia had been speaking to him infuriated Etakai.

"I'm going to bed," Alia called back. "We can talk another time."

"Shall I alert the guards of your guest?" The man's tone was sly. "I saw him creep in through your window. Instead of alerting the guards I decided to confront you both myself, like the good old days."

Etakai clenched his fists.

Alia was shocked the wood had not burst into flames because of his glare.

"Let him in," Etakai muttered.

Alia went to the door and unlocked it, then pulled it open. "Please don't tell anyone, Clyde," she whispered as the man stepped into the room and shut the door behind him.

Clyde had short hair that was dark red and eyes that were almost black. A scar that reached from his nose across his cheek was one he had received from Etakai. He wore a cloak and armor. Like his father before him, Clyde was the Captain of the Guard.

"Etakai," said Clyde darkly

"Clyde," Etakai replied.

Alia looked between them with worry. She knew the two of them had an unpleasant history.

Clyde claimed Etakai had killed his father and held a grudge for it. Etakai in turn believed Clyde had known his father, Marcus, was part of the group that killed Fasentario and hated him for being mad that Etakai got his revenge. They had fought, which resulted in Etakai cutting Clyde's face.

The static between them was smothering.

"I'm busy tonight, Clyde," said Etakai. "If you don't mind, I'd love to get out of here before we're all discovered."

Clyde smirked. "I'm not letting you get away." He drew his sword. "Not this time."

"Don't fight in here," Alia hissed.

Neither of them paid her any mind.

Etakai slipped three knives from his belt. "Should I try asking again?"

"There would be no point."

"Pity."

Clyde spun his sword just in time to ricochet one of Etakai's throwing knives. He lunged at Etakai to close the distance between them, slashing back and forth and then delivering a vertical cut that could have killed Etakai, but Etakai crossed two of his throwing knives and deflected the blade.

He slid back and Clyde came at him again.

Alia pressed her back against the door with her bag clutched tight.

Clyde lunged at Etakai who jumped sideways, landed with his feet on the wall, then flipped, landing in a handstand on Clyde's shoulders.

"Am I too much for you?" Etakai teased, looking at Clyde upside-down.

"No," said Clyde with a smirk. "You're just right."

Etakai saw Clyde draw the hidden knife an instant too late.

The blade slammed straight through his collar. He screamed as he crashed to the ground–

Etakai's eyes flew open.

He was panting and his entire body ached. His chest was wrapped in bandages, beneath which were three knife wounds that had nearly killed him.

As the dream faded from his mind, he

remembered where he was. It was the Real World. He had been removed from his story a few days ago, though to him it felt like years.

The rumbling sound of cars on the street outside confirmed his thought.

Through the curtains, sunlight streamed into the room. Etakai blinked in the light and lifted his head a little. He was on a large bed with the covers drawn up to his chin. The room was fashionable and well furnished. Etakai let his head fall back into the pillows with a curse.

He hated the Real World.

Chapter Six
Bad Memories

"How long has it been since I've dreamed of my past?" Etakai wondered, lifting a bandaged hand to wipe sweat off his forehead. He let his fingers draw an X on his cheek beneath his left eye. The fang tattoo had left scars on his face. The faint X would fade, but he could still feel it.

The memories of the night he attacked everyone rushed to his mind.

It had happened on the street outside Reitrin's apartment. Thinking back, Etakai saw Fevros catch his throwing knives and then throw them back. He felt the sting of the blades buried in his chest, then the darkness overtook him and he heard shouting, saw green fire, and knew nothing of what he was doing until he felt something wrap around him.

Something warm and safe.

Reitrin had spoken to him. Her voice had drawn him back to reality. He had looked at her, seeing she was a mess like him. She had asked if he was okay. No. He hadn't been. Next thing he knew he had blacked out again.

Now, Etakai let his hand lay on his forehead as he watched the ceiling. They must have brought him here. How was he alive? The knife wounds in his chest should have killed him.

It was similar to the night his parents died.

Perhaps the green fire and Reitrin's kindness had brought back his memories? He lost control back then too.

Etakai watched the ceiling fan as it rotated above him. How much time had passed since he blacked out? His mind was troubled. How many people had he hurt when he went berserk? What if it happened again?

He could end up killing the others.

Etakai wished he had been left in his story, if only to remain ignorant of the other worlds and storybook characters like him. He also wished he knew why he had been removed from his novel and left in the Real World. Just what had the Eysheus named Aoiro stood to gain?

A sneer crossed Etakai's face. An Eysheus was a person that could enter and manipulate storybooks at will. Etakai wished he were strong enough to punch Aoiro in the face, but the man and his red fire were too powerful.

There came a knock on the door and Etakai heaved a sigh of annoyance.

"Who is it?" he called. A twinge of pain in his chest made him wince.

The door opened and Reitrin looked in at him. Her brown eyes lit up when he met her gaze.

"I'm glad you're awake," she said, walking into the room and sitting on the bed beside him. Her short hair had been freshly cut and styled.

"Before you ask," said Reitrin, holding up her hand. "You've been unconscious for a week."

Etakai was alarmed. "A week?"

"Yes. It seems like you're finally regaining some color in your face though." Reitrin frowned at him. "Your skin looked gray for so long. I was frightened.

Hiro said not to worry, but I ..." she stopped and coughed. "Well, I was annoyed that I had to babysit you for an entire week."

Etakai rolled his eyes. She didn't want to admit she had been scared to lose him.

"Shan has been hunting for a new location for his restaurant," Reitrin said, looking out the window. "He found a place yesterday and wanted me to tell you about it as soon as you woke up."

"How is he doing?" Etakai asked.

"He has cheered up," Reitrin replied. "After Fevros blew up the street and you went berserk he was jumpy and quiet for a few days. He's almost back to his old self now."

"Not sure if that's a good thing," Etakai groaned. Shan could be too bubbly sometimes.

"The building is huge," Reitrin explained. Her happy mood faded a little. "The downstairs used to be a bar, and the upstairs was used as living quarters, so there is space for all of us to stay there if we want."

Etakai grinned. "So, we'll live in The Hideaway?"

"Above it, technically," Reitrin grumbled.

"You don't want to live with all of us?" Etakai could have laughed. Reitrin had been housing them since the day he showed up in the Real World. Her apartment was ruined after Fevros blew open the street so she should have been happy to have a new place to stay.

"It's going to require a lot of work before we can live there," Reitrin explained. "Everything is dusty and old."

"And?"

"And Shan said Sia could stay there too."

Bingo. Reitrin didn't want her older sister mooching off Shan. Now Etakai knew why she looked grumpy.

It was time to change the subject.

"Have you spoken to the prince much?" Etakai's grin became one of mockery. He saw Reitrin look away from him, her cheeks flushed.

"No," she muttered. "He's always out of sight, but I can feel him watching me."

"I bet."

Reitrin shot him a glare.

Etakai chuckled then cut off when it hurt. He was amused because the prince he spoke of was actually a wannabe king named Xitou from the storybook *The Lord of Desolation*. Inside the book, Reitrin had met Xitou and developed feelings for him.

"You seem like you're feeling better." Reitrin gazed out the window at the blue sky. There were puffy white clouds rolling by and a jet left a white stream.

"I'm sore and tired," muttered Etakai, looking out the window too. "I had a dream about my past."

Reitrin glanced at him. "A good dream?"

Etakai shook his head with a frown. "My green fire … I've done all of this before."

Reitrin touched her arms when he said this. Etakai knew under her long-sleeved shirt she wore bandages. The green fire had burned them both when he lost control; he had seen the burns on her before he blacked out.

Etakai frowned, but then lifted his hand and looked at his fingertips. They were all he could see beneath the bandages and they, too, were red from burns.

"I went crazy when my parents were murdered."

Reitrin stared at him. "Murdered?"

Etakai nodded and lowered his hand over his face. "Reitrin."

"Yes?"

"If this happens again ..." He hesitated, but then shook his head. "No, never mind."

Reitrin watched him sadly. "Are you hungry?"

Etakai shook his head.

"At least take some water. Hiro said you're dehydrated."

Etakai scowled, then nodded.

Reitrin left to get the water and Etakai glared at the ceiling.

Hiro, formally known as Hirochi, was a man who was mostly machine. He was hundreds of years old but didn't look a day over thirty.

Etakai did not enjoy his memory of Hiro. The night he went berserk, Hiro had been prepared to kill him, and he would have, if Reitrin hadn't intervened.

Hiro was also Chief of the Secret Police, and Etakai had a feeling they would be meeting again soon, since he had nearly killed his men.

"I kind of wish I had died," Etakai muttered as he shut his eyes.

Chapter Seven
Things of the Past

Reitrin worked hard to dust and clean Shan's new building. It hurt her burns to move so much.

The bar was long, sitting between the kitchen door and the door to the stairs, and Shan had purchased metal stools to bolt into the floor that had soft dark red cushions and backrest. The dark red cushions helped them match the round redwood tables and chairs sitting in the corner waiting to be set out.

It was a large space with plenty of room for customers. Reitrin liked the front doors the most. They were two large Victorian glass doors that, once cleaned, had gold details in the glass and golden handles.

The building was on a corner, with windows looking out onto the street. A wooden awning wrapped the outside of their building and Shan was pleased to have "The Hideaway" affixed above the awning in gold letters. It had been expensive and Reitrin, who was somehow stuck tallying their budget, was angry at Shan for buying the letters without her permission, but when she looked at the restaurant from across the street she was satisfied.

It looked much more welcoming than his old café, and it was in the middle of town, two blocks from the library, five from the hospital, and three from the police station. All of which were locations storybook characters were drawn to.

Reitrin could look down the street and see roads she had not walked down since she was younger.

The grocery store she frequented was also nearby, which would be good for making last-minute runs for the restaurant. And down the alley, at the back, there was a garage.

Shan had already begun pricing out cars, but Reitrin warned him that they would need to make a lot of money in the restaurant before they could buy something so expensive.

"Don't you have a car?" Shan asked when Reitrin pulled the car magazine out of his hands.

"It's my dad's," Reitrin grumbled as she threw the magazine away. She sighed and looked around at the dusty rafters she had yet to clean.

Thinking about her missing father depressed her. All the chances she had to speak to Aoiro, and she had not asked about her father's health or whereabouts.

He hadn't been a great father to her. Since he blamed Reitrin for the death of his wife he had only tolerated her. When her older sister Sia moved out, their father had treated Reitrin like a servant and bullied her. He had never raised a hand against her, but he called her a murderer often enough to damage Reitrin's image of herself.

When she thought about it, part of Reitrin didn't care that Aoiro had taken him. But she wondered why he had.

Aoiro, the redheaded Eysheus, had been a serious pain. Twice he held Reitrin captive and then let her escape. He was powerful enough he could have stopped her, but he hadn't. He was also the reason

Reitrin had been able to save Etakai from being killed in a poorly written historical fiction novel.

It felt like months ago, but it had only been a week. Reitrin shivered. She didn't want to go into any more books, but she knew it was not wise to hope for it. Not since she was friends with a fictional character.

Reitrin wondered if Etakai would be okay. She knew nothing of his story, except that he was supposed to be the hero, but he rarely acted like one. She lowered the rag which she had been dusting the bar shelves with.

Just what was his story about?

"Shan," said Reitrin as Shan used a broom to wipe cobwebs off the rafters. There were crystal lights hanging from golden chains and Shan was trying to free them from the dust. He was short so the task was taking a lot of effort. "You read Etakai's story, right?"

Shan stopped working and lowered the broom. He hesitated, then looked back at Reitrin. There was dust on his face and glasses. "I guess?"

"You guess?" Reitrin pressed.

Shan took off his glasses and brushed the dust out of his unruly black hair. "I don't remember the book."

"You don't remember it?"

"I remember there was a book and it was Etakai's," explained Shan, frowning at his glasses. "I also know I hadn't finished reading it before it disappeared. But other than that I don't remember anything about it. When I met Etakai I knew all about his story, but now there's nothing in my memory. I don't even remember what the cover looked like."

Reitrin stared at him. "Are you serious?"

Shan nodded.

Reitrin was shocked. She wondered if Etakai's story had turned to dust. The last book they had entered was gone. Reitrin couldn't recall anything about the book except Flamelord, who had thrown his sword at her and almost killed her, and Ace, the man she had saved by taking the sword for him.

No matter how hard she tried to recall the name of the book she drew a blank. Everything was gone from her memory.

The world of storybooks was frightening.

"Do you think it's … gone?" Reitrin hesitated to ask this.

"I don't know," replied Shan grimly. "Etakai is still here. Maybe the book is okay?"

Reitrin shrugged. It was true that Etakai had not turned to dust, but was that because he was in the Real World?

"Would Hiro know?" Reitrin wondered.

"If he comes by we could ask him," said Shan with a sigh. "The Secret Police deal specifically with book jumpers, so I'm sure he could answer a lot of our questions."

Reitrin stood in silence for a moment longer before continuing to work. She had spent her week back in the Real World caring for Etakai and helping Shan hunt for a new restaurant. And keeping Sia out of the bars.

Sia, her older sister, would drink whenever she felt stressed. After all she had witnessed, she was unable to keep herself from the bars.

The first time Reitrin let her out of her sight Sia had been gone all night and showed up in their hotel with a large tab from the bar down the street. Reitrin had scolded her, since she now had to pay for Sia's drinking as well as the painkillers that she, Shan, and Etakai needed, all while managing Shan's restaurant expenses.

Reitrin took out her frustration on the cobwebs under the counter.

A hard day's work later, Reitrin was permitted to leave. She was working as Shan's employee and he insisted she only cleaned during her work hours, though it was volunteer work until the restaurant opened.

Shan was a surprisingly strict boss. If Reitrin was late then she worked late, and if her break was too long then she had to make up for that too. Shan was tough. It was like he was two different people: the kind man she was friends with, and the strict businessman that owned The Hideaway, and ran it with an iron fist.

Reitrin packed up her things and went back to the hotel. It was a long walk in the gathering darkness, but Reitrin knew she was not alone.

"Xitou," she said to the empty street behind her. "Are you going to hide from me forever?"

There was no reply.

The street lights flickered to life and Reitrin slowed down. She was near the hotel; she could see the large white walls and the parking lot with only a handful of cars parked. This wasn't what slowed Reitrin.

Beneath the street light ahead of her was a

familiar man.

Xitou looked regal wearing the black clothes of the Secret Police. His long black hair was tied back and the scar over his eye was partially hidden by an eye patch. The sword that hung at his hip would raise eyebrows. Xitou was not the only member of the Secret Police that wore such weapons though.

"I am not hiding from you," he said when Reitrin came up to him. He stood beneath a streetlight with his arms crossed. Though the ugly scar showed above and below his eye patch, Reitrin did not mind it. She watched Xitou's calm brown eye that held her gaze.

"You left my story before I could save you," Xitou muttered.

"I had no control over that," Reitrin told him. "Aoiro sent us out because he said the book was dying." She was finding it difficult to speak.

Seeing Xitou again, in the Real World, in modern clothing, was almost too much for her to bear. She had been able to imagine him as a fictional character in her mind. In her memory it was like a dream that had faded. She could separate him from her reality. But now he was much too real.

"Give your excuses," Xitou retorted. "It was not fair. I had abandoned my own mission to help your friend save you and I was utterly useless. And then you left before I had a chance to do anything about it."

"But in the end it worked out, didn't it?" Reitrin saw the pain cross Xitou's face, and she realized she had said the wrong thing.

"The fate of my storybook hangs in the balance," Xitou told her. He looked down the street to the hotel with grief etched on his face. "Thankfully, the Secret Police are able to hold it immobile so it won't die while I am away."

"Is that going to be a while?"

Xitou glanced down at Reitrin who watched him with a hint of color on her cheeks.

"Perhaps," Xitou replied.

For a moment they watched each other.

Reitrin looked away and coughed into her sleeve. "I need to get back to check on Etakai. I hope Sia hasn't invaded another bar."

"Hiro has given her a strict guard to keep her from the drinks," Xitou explained. "One who drinks will likely tell tales, and we cannot have her blabbing about all she has seen. She's a risk to our safety."

Reitrin felt relieved, but also scared. Sia was a sly person when she wanted to be. The Secret Police would have been wiser to lock her up to keep her from causing trouble.

"Shall I escort you like a normal person?" Xitou inquired as he offered his arm.

"Normal?" Reitrin laughed. "That's not normal."

"I meant, allow me to escort you in person instead of following you in the shadows," Xitou corrected. He walked away without waiting for an answer.

Reitrin hurried after him and slipped her arm in his.

Xitou gave her a surprised look, but Reitrin avoided meeting his gaze as a blush crossed her face.

They walked back to the hotel and took the elevator to the second floor. Reitrin's room was down the narrow halls. A guest of the hotel passed them and gave the two of them a bewildered look as he went.

"I suppose I am not capable of reaching the 'normal' mark in your world," Xitou grumbled as Reitrin took a card key from her pocket to open the door.

"No, but that's okay," she said. The door beeped and she pushed it open.

Inside was a living room with a small kitchen attached. There was one bedroom with two beds and a couch where Shan slept. Reitrin and Sia shared one bed while Etakai, who had been unconscious up until that morning, had a bed to himself.

"I need to keep on patrol," said Xitou, remaining outside the doorway.

Reitrin looked back at him. "Oh. Okay."

"I'm never too far," he told her, trying to grin, but failing.

They were both silent again, but then Xitou heaved a sigh.

"When we were last together, the circumstances were ugly," he said, shifting his weight and leaning his arm on the door frame. He looked up and down the hallway with an uncomfortable expression. "I called you a bad omen. That monster had attacked the camp and then that strange man, Fevros, made me angry. I took it out on you, but I regretted it as soon as you were gone from sight."

"It's okay," Reitrin tried to say, but Xitou was shaking his head.

"No, it's not," he said, lifting his eye to look at her. "Reitrin, you are not a bad omen. Trouble is following you, but you're not to blame."

"I ..." Reitrin's mouth was dry, but then she

stepped forward into the hallway, facing Xitou who appeared to be holding his breath. "I don't think that's true."

"What do you mean?" Xitou whispered. The door shut behind her and she stood so close they almost touched.

"I mean," Reitrin explained slowly. "I managed to remove Etakai and myself from the history book. I did that, Xitou. I just … I just willed us out, and we were out."

Xitou drew back, staring at her as if he had only realized she was there.

Reitrin did not like the look. "What's wrong? Is that a bad thing?"

"You're from the Real World," Xitou replied. "That shouldn't be possible."

"So it is bad." Reitrin looked away from him. "I knew it. I shouldn't have told anyone."

"No, it's for the best," said Xitou as he stepped away from her. "I have to tell Hiro about this."

"Can't you keep it a secret?" Reitrin insisted.

Xitou shook his head. "I'm sorry, but it may have something to do with why you were involved in the first place. I'm glad you told me."

Reitrin wanted to say more, but Xitou turned on his heel and strode away. Even after he was gone, Reitrin stood immobile in front of the doorway. She felt cold and scared. Xitou was about to tell Hiro what she had not wanted to tell anyone.

She bit her lip, but then turned and opened the door again. Inside, she locked the door and looked for signs of Sia.

There were no extra shoes lying around and no

jacket or socks on the floor. Sia must not have come back yet.

Reitrin rubbed her tired eyes and went to the bedroom to check on Etakai. The lights were off, but the orange glow of sunset illuminated Etakai's pale face and bandages.

"Sia still isn't back," Reitrin murmured as she went to the window.

"She was here earlier," grumbled Etakai.

Reitrin glanced back at him. His eyes were still shut. "Did I wake you?"

"Yes," Etakai murmured. "But that's good. It means I'm healthy enough to wake when someone enters the room."

"But not before," Reitrin said with a grin.

Etakai sighed without response.

Reitrin looked back out the window. "Shan wants the restaurant to open by the end of the month. I was hoping you would be well enough by then to help out."

"Perhaps." Etakai's voice was quiet. He was still sleepy.

Reitrin closed the curtains. "I'm sorry I woke you," she said as she went to the door.

"Reitrin," Etakai said, making Reitrin pause. "I can hear your sister. She's coming up the stairs, but she's not alone."

"Thanks," said Reitrin. She left the room, making sure to shut the door behind her. If Sia wasn't alone then that was not a good sign.

The door beeped and Reitrin watched it open.

Sia peeked inside. Her long blond hair was in a braid and her clothes were fashionable. She looked pale though and Reitrin raised an eyebrow at her.

"Hey," said Sia quietly. "Are you alone?"

"Yes," replied Reitrin. "Why are you acting weird?"

As an answer, Sia pushed open the door, revealing the man behind her who wore a hood and held a gun to Sia's head.

"Because this man wants to speak to you in private," Sia squeaked. "And it's urgent."

Chapter Eight
The Unwelcome Guest

Reitrin stood paralyzed with shock. The hooded stranger stepped into the hotel room and kicked the door shut behind him.

"He wants you to close the curtains," Sia said.

Reitrin glanced over her shoulder at the window looking at the buildings beside the hotel. She glanced once at the stranger, but then went to the curtains and drew them shut.

"Should I offer you tea or water?" Reitrin asked, turning back to the stranger.

He wore a long black cloak. His boots were also dark, but filthy with mud. The cloak, as well as his dark gloves, looked old and frayed. Up close it was clear the cloak was ancient and so was the bow and quiver the man carried. Inside the quiver were black-shafted arrows. Reitrin's heart shuddered in her chest.

"Are you going to tell me who you are?" Reitrin asked. She remained by the window and tried hard not to look towards the bedroom door. She hoped Etakai was listening.

The man lowered the gun from Sia's head, but then disassembled it and threw the pieces aside.

"I am known as Traitor," the man said.

Reitrin gave a start. His voice was angelic. She had never heard a man with such a kind voice before and it threw off his appearance.

"Traitor?" Reitrin repeated. She looked at Sia,

who cautiously moved away from the man.

"Do you need to sit down?" Reitrin motioned Traitor to the open couch and chairs. "You look like you've been through a lot."

"I have," Traitor replied with gravity. "I heard you are a hero. You saved a man named Ace from being impaled, is this true?"

Reitrin nodded and her hand touched her abdomen. There was a pale scar there, and an identical one on her back. Flamelord's sword had gone straight through her. The only reason she was alive was because of Etakai, and someone else that had secretly given her storybook herbs to save her.

At least that was what the Eysheus Aoiro had told her. Reitrin was not sure if she could trust him. He claimed he was a villain but did not act like one all the time, so Reitrin did not know what to believe.

"I need help," said Traitor. "The woman I love has been taken captive and is being used as leverage to make me do terrible things."

"You look as if doing terrible things should be second nature," Reitrin told him, crossing her arms. Her burns stung from working and she wished the man had not shown up. She desperately wanted to put on some salve to ease the pain and then go to bed.

"I was written this way for good reason," the man told her with a hint of spite. "I was removed from the near end of my story, so I am not as murderous as I once was. You must help me, young hero. The girl I want you to save is my light. She is the one who must save me. Without her I am doomed to the darkest of deaths and I am also at the mercy of the Eysheus."

Reitrin glanced at Sia who had sunk to the ground in the kitchen and was holding herself as if she were cold.

"What's the girl's name?" Reitrin asked, looking back at Traitor.

"Wyvetta." Traitor spoke her name as if it was precious to him. "She is not a fighter, but she is a survivor. Please, I cannot save her on my own. If I do anything wrong, she will be killed and my book will dissolve."

"Where is she being kept?"

"The Real World."

Reitrin gawked at the man. "The Real World? You mean she may be in this city?"

"The one who took her resides in this city," Traitor answered, "though he, too, is fictional. Please, just tell me if you will help. I am running out of time. I had only a small window to escape the watch of the Eysheus and come find you."

Reitrin gently rubbed her arms. "Do you mind if I ask for help with this?"

"No, I do not," replied Traitor. "I only came to you because you sacrificed yourself for another. Only one who does such selfless things can be trusted to save my light."

Reitrin heaved a sigh. "Then I'll help. Do you have any information for me on how I may find her?"

"Yes," replied Traitor. "There lies a desolate fortress on the edge of this city. In that fortress you will find her. Now, I am out of time." He took an arrow, notched it, and then turned and shot it at Sia who screamed and lurched away.

The arrow pierced the wall, but not before cutting

Sia's arm.

"What did you do that for?" Reitrin barked.

Traitor retrieved the arrow, making Sia scurry away from him.

"Blood and fear must remain when I leave," he said as he went to the door. "Anything else is suspicious." He threw the door open and left.

When the door shut the atmosphere lightened and Reitrin felt as if she could finally breathe.

"Oh. My. God!" Sia was holding her hand to her chest. She was turning gray and trembling everywhere.

Reitrin looked at her and realized she was having a panic attack. She went to her sister and knelt beside her. "Breathe, Sia. Just breathe." She rubbed her sister's arm, trying to help her calm down.

Their mother used to hold Sia and sing to her when she had panic attacks. That had calmed Sia down almost instantly, but Reitrin was not their mother.

The bedroom door opened and Reitrin looked up in surprise.

Etakai stood leaning on the door frame, holding his hand over his chest. He was white as a sheet and covered in bandages with only dark gray pajama pants on.

"What are you doing up?" Reitrin demanded.

"Oh, come on," grumbled Etakai, glaring across the room at her. "I'm not letting you go find that Wyvetta girl alone."

"You're in no condition for more adventures," Reitrin shot back. "You can hardly stand. Get back to bed."

Etakai scowled, but then teetered backwards and only just managed to catch himself on the door frame.

"You two will be the death of me!" Reitrin cried as she left Sia and ran to help Etakai get back into bed. "I'm not a nurse for pity's sake."

"No, you're just dependable," Etakai grumbled.

"You say that like it's a bad thing."

"It is," muttered Etakai. "Because you're going after that girl, but … I can't let you go alone."

"I'll speak to Hiro in the morning and see if he can help me." Reitrin helped Etakai back into his bed. "It's storybook related and I'm sure he'll be thrilled to deal with me again."

She turned to go, but Etakai caught her wrist and pulled her back.

"Be careful," he whispered, gazing up at her.

Reitrin stared at him. "Y…yeah, I will." She slid her wrist from his grip and then left to check on Sia.

Chapter Nine
About Being a Hero

Birds were chirping in the trees along the street as Reitrin made her way towards the library. She knew nothing about the man called Traitor and was worried she had taken on a job she could not handle. He was working for an Eysheus, being blackmailed into doing as he was told, but it was all because his girl was in danger. Reitrin hoped she could find their book to learn a little more about them, but there was a chance the book would be missing like Etakai's.

"I don't know what I'm doing," Reitrin admitted to herself as she climbed the stairs to the library.

"About time she spoke," said a voice behind her.

Reitrin whipped around. She was alarmed to find Xitou and Hiro were following her. They stood two steps behind her. How had she not heard them?

"Her awareness is not impressive," said Hiro as he turned to walk away. "If she were a storybook character she would have sensed us."

"That's not the only way to tell," Xitou offered to Hiro's retreating back. "Not all storybook characters can sense followers. She used magic, Chief. Isn't this worth an investigation?"

"No. I don't have time to waste, prince, but you insisted we trail her to see if she shows signs of storybook world magic. I saw nothing, so I'm leaving."

"But she used magic." Xitou clenched his jaw. "Why won't you investigate?"

Hiro didn't answer.

"Hold on, Hiro," Reitrin called, making Hiro stop to look back at her. "Someone called Traitor just came to my hotel to ask me for help."

Hiro watched her, but then faced Xitou. "Did you know of this?"

"No," replied Xitou.

"You left your post for a few seconds to talk to me and she was contacted by the enemy," Hiro growled. "Dammit, they move fast."

"I thought Malakavel would cover for me," Xitou grumbled. "I asked him to before I left."

"If you do not get a direct 'yes' from him, then he is not going to help." Hiro turned to Reitrin. "Did this man mention any names? Perhaps of the one that removed him from his book, or what his book was?"

"No, nothing like that," Reitrin replied. "He said he only had a small window to speak to me, so he was brief. He wants me to–"

Hiro's hand snapped up, silencing Reitrin.

"She is not impressive," Hiro said to Xitou.

"Why do you keep saying that?" Reitrin asked.

"Xitou thinks you're some kind of spectacular person," Hiro said as he walked away. "But you don't watch your back and you speak of sensitive things out in the street." He stopped at the bottom of the stairs, looking back at the two of them. "We're going to headquarters. We can speak freely there. Come with me."

As he left, Xitou looked back at Reitrin. She met his gaze, glanced at the library behind her, then hurried after Hiro.

Hiro brought them down the street and stopped

beside a black sedan with dark windows. He unlocked the doors and opened the back door for Reitrin who hesitated before crawling inside. The door shut behind her. She clasped her hands and looked around the tan interior. It was clean and smelled like roses with a hint of old blood.

Hiro took the driver's side and Xitou awkwardly sat in the passenger's seat beside him.

"These things are weird," Xitou told Reitrin as Hiro started the engine.

"As are you, prince," replied Hiro as he checked the road and pulled out of his parking place.

"I'm a king," Xitou replied sourly.

"No, you're supposed to be a king," Hiro told him. "Until you have your precious jewel and a crown on your head, I will call you prince."

Xitou slouched back in the chair with a scowl.

Reitrin gazed out the window as they drove down the twisting roads. They left the city, heading up a slope towards a small park where a lonely bench sat. Someone had left roses on it.

Hiro pulled over near the bench. There was a turnaround ahead of them surrounded by bushes and trees. Hiro dropped the visor, revealing a thin strip with buttons on it. Reitrin watched with interest as Hiro tapped a few of them and then pushed the visor back up.

The road trembled beneath the car. The center of the turnaround split open, revealing a second road that proceeded down into the hill.

Hiro drove slowly down the slope. Once they were clear, the ground slid shut above them. Reitrin looked back and saw blinking red lights on the back of the massive steel doors.

"This is incredible," Reitrin whispered.

"You didn't think we kept our headquarters out in the open, did you?" Hiro asked, flipping on the headlights to reveal the road, which led down to a steel wall with narrow windows and doors. It was a tall structure built into the cavern wall. There were soft blue lights illuminating the walls, the street, and the sentries who stood guard at the large gate that stood at the bottom of the road.

Hiro pulled up to the sentries, stopping before the gate. When he rolled down his window, Reitrin had to catch her breath. The man who went to the window wore the uniform of the Secret Police, but his face was twisted, he was short, and his skin seemed unhealthy.

"Welcome back, Chief," said the man, his voice deep and gurgling. The second sentry remained away from them, holding his rifle at the ready.

"You're looking off, Jekyll," said Hiro, showing the man his ID. "Any trouble today?"

"No," grumbled the man as he waved to the second sentry who pulled a lever to open the gate. "Too early."

"No such thing," said Hiro, pocketing his ID as the gate slid open. He drove through and Reitrin stared at Jekyll as they passed him.

"I think I've heard of him," she said.

"We're about to enter a place where there are many storybook characters, Ms. Nichol," said Hiro as he pulled up to the steel wall. The front door of the station was also steel with a blinking light in the center. "Please do us all a favor and keep your head."

Reitrin nodded.

Hiro stepped out and opened the door for her. Reitrin found she was trembling with excitement as she slid out of the car and looked up at the high ceiling. From somewhere in the cave, she could hear the rushing of a waterfall.

Reitrin walked with Hiro and Xitou to the front door, which slid open as soon as Hiro was close. Reitrin could have sworn she heard something inside Hiro beep before the door opened, but she wondered if it had been her imagination.

As soon as they entered, Reitrin's ears were filled with the buzz of activity. She stood in a long white hallway with many doors, most of which were open for people to come and go. The people inside wore white or black uniforms and many of them held clipboards or cell phones. A few people were dressed in scrubs.

"Chief!" a woman called across the hall. She had thick curly hair, pure black with gold streaks, and bright red eyes. "We have a request for backup in the next state over. Their jumper is lethal."

"Send what they need," said Hiro, leading Xitou and Reitrin through the chaos.

"Chief." A man with thick glasses and no hair fell into step with Hiro and showed him a clipboard. "We have requests made to purchase this weapon, but it needs your signature–"

"Too much for too little," said Hiro, glancing once at the paper. "Denied." He waved the man away only to be joined by another woman asking if he was okay with sending a response team to some place across the ocean.

Reitrin was speechless and felt dizzy from all the people bothering Hiro and how calmly he sorted their problems and moved on to the next. It continued until he reached the end of the hall and two giant glass doors slid open at the top of a platform that overlooked a room filled with computers and people working. The buzzing was louder in here.

"The delivery arrived this morning," a woman told Hiro as she walked past them, going into the hallway while tucking a pen behind her ear.

"Thank you," said Hiro, his golden eyes searching the room. He scowled then motioned to the left for Xitou and Reitrin.

They took the stairs down to a plain wood door that had a strange mechanical device on it. It beeped at Hiro and swung open.

Inside there was an office with a nice wood desk, painted black, a rolling chair, and two armchairs on the other side. At the back of the room there was also a short brown sofa.

"No unexpected visitors," Hiro told the door. It beeped in reply.

Hiro held the door for Xitou and Reitrin who slipped inside with cautious looks at the door.

Once they were inside, Hiro let the door snap shut behind him and a dinging sound filled the room. It ended when Hiro snapped his fingers.

"What was that?" Reitrin asked.

"What was what?" Hiro asked as he sank into his rolling chair behind the desk.

Reitrin blinked at him. She had no idea where to start after all she had just seen, so she simply sank into one of the armchairs and left her question unanswered.

"The first thing you need to learn about acting as a hero is you are not meant to work alone," Hiro told Reitrin, leaning back in his chair. "Now, I believe you were telling us a story?"

Reitrin blinked. She had no idea what he was talking about, but then it clicked, and she gave a start.

"Yes, I was!" she proclaimed.

Xitou placed his hand over his face.

Hiro frowned at Xitou. "You were even more perplexed than she when you first came here, prince. At least she knows what cars, sliding doors, and colored lights are."

Xitou scowled at the ground.

Reitrin hunched her shoulders, but with Hiro's calm wave, she fell into the story of Traitor showing up with a gun to her sister's head and everything that transpired between them. She finished her story and watched Hiro, waiting for a reply.

Hiro was quiet for a long time. He stood up and left the office without a word.

Reitrin stared after him with shock.

Xitou also looked surprised.

Reitrin turned to Xitou. "Did I offend him?"

"No, I don't think that would make him leave the room," Xitou told her. "He would only look at you as if you were scum and tell you never to say something like that again."

Reitrin frowned. "You sound like you know that for sure. Did you say something to offend him before?"

"Yes."

The conversation died and they watched the

door, waiting for Hiro to return.

"Is Etakai well?"

Reitrin glanced at Xitou who crossed his arms. His jaw was clenched.

"Yeah," replied Reitrin. "Why?"

Xitou shrugged. "You were so worried about him that you were in a rush to return. It seems to me like he's more important to you than he used to be."

Reitrin opened her mouth to respond when the door opened and two people entered. One was Hiro, and the other was a stranger with dark red hair who wore a black cloak, which was pulled back over one shoulder to display the plated armor on his arms and legs and chain-mail beneath a dark leather tunic. His eyes were black and he looked Reitrin up and down with distaste. A pale scar ran from his nose across his cheek.

"Since you are here asking for help, I have brought some," said Hiro, returning to his chair behind his desk. The door snapped shut behind the new arrival. "I am sure only a few introductions are needed." Hiro leaned back to look at the company in front of him. "Xitou knows you, correct?"

"Yes," said the man. His voice was deep.

Xitou also nodded and shrank away from the newcomer. Reitrin couldn't blame him. The stranger had a dominant presence.

"Reitrin," said Hiro. "Meet Clyde, Captain of the Guard. He is from Etakai's world."

Reitrin stared at Clyde in alarm. "Etakai's world? Are you serious?"

"Clyde," continued Hiro, ignoring Reitrin's reaction. "This young lady is Reitrin Nichol, the

Eysheus wannabe."

"Charmed," Clyde said, examining Reitrin again. His gaze was so sturdy it made her uncomfortable.

"According to Reitrin, a man named Traitor claims a girl called Wyvetta is being kept hostage in the Real World," Hiro explained to Clyde. "He told her the girl was being kept in a fortress. Do you think you could figure out where he means?"

"It will take some searching," murmured Clyde. "Now that the black clouds are gone, I can't wander as freely as I used to. And it will also be harder for me to work if I'm stuck with this useless girl." He jabbed his thumb at Reitrin.

"She's not useless," said Xitou.

Clyde cast Xitou a look of such loathing it even made Reitrin feel small.

"Clyde, we're comrades here," said Hiro, folding his arms. "Accept that now or I'll take you off this mission and stick you on guard duty with Sydran."

Clyde's expression glazed over as if the thought of working with Sydran was enough to kill him. "Heaven protect me from that nuisance," he whispered, passing his hand over his face. "As you wish, Chief."

"Good, so get going," said Hiro. "I have an appointment with Intelligence. They may know more about Traitor and his story, so keep your phones on."

"Yes, sir," said Xitou. "We'll report if we find anything."

"Good," replied Hiro. "And don't forget, Reitrin is leading this mission. You two are just her bodyguards."

Reitrin was startled by this. "Are you sure that's

a good idea?"

Hiro's golden eyes locked on hers. "Traitor came to you, and you need to learn how to watch your back. Xitou and Clyde will help you with that. They are both noble knights in their stories."

"Don't drag me down to this scum's level," Clyde growled, giving Xitou a death glare.

"Clyde," Hiro said in a dangerous tone.

"I understand," Clyde grumbled, looking away.

"Then go," said Hiro, waving to the door, "Before you make me late for my next appointment."

Chapter Ten
Command

Reitrin was brought around to the back of the hideout. She learned it was much bigger than she had imagined. There were two garages on either side of the main building with an assortment of vehicles and more than five exits that she noticed. Some tunnels led to neighboring towns, and Xitou told her others led to underwater docks that were used to reach other countries.

The operation of the Secret Police was so widespread it boggled Reitrin's mind that they managed to keep themselves as hidden as they did.

Xitou and Clyde selected a gray four-door SUV with tinted windows with a blue dash light. Reitrin was startled to see Clyde was the one who would be driving. In his cloak and medieval armor he did not look like he would know how to drive a vehicle of the Real World.

"How long have the Secret Police been around?" Reitrin wondered as she climbed into the passenger's seat beside Clyde.

"Decades," replied Clyde. "Maybe a century or two. Hirochi founded it. Ask him."

Reitrin gawked at him. She had known Hiro was a machine that did not age, but she hadn't expected him to be over a hundred years old.

"How long have you been a part of it?"

Clyde shrugged. "My time has been on and off. I had missions back in my story, so I have lost track of my time in the Real World."

"I thought you would be more tight-lipped," Reitrin told him as he started the vehicle.

Xitou climbed into the back seat and shut his door. "He's only tight-lipped when it suits him."

Clyde scowled at him through the rear-view mirror.

"Whatever it is that makes you two hate each other, can you forget it for now?" Reitrin asked, looking from one to the other.

"It was just hate at first sight," said Xitou bitterly.

"It's more than that for me," Clyde growled under his breath, but he said no more as he put the car in gear and drove off through the dark tunnel.

The road they traveled twisted around then went up a tight slope. Clyde tapped some buttons on the dashboard similar to the strip on the visor of Hiro's sedan, and above them a trap door slid open. Bright sunlight glared on the windshield.

"A fortress on the edge of the city is all we have to go on," Clyde said, as if speaking to himself.

"It will probably be guarded," Reitrin mused as she watched houses and trees fly past the car. They were on a road near the city limit that was mostly parking lots and old businesses. "I don't know of any fortresses out here."

"Most storybook characters have to use descriptions from their own world to describe this world," Clyde explained. "A fortress to Traitor could be any type of large building made of bricks or stone."

Reitrin snapped her fingers. "The abandoned

factory." She looked at Clyde. "Out past the old industrial park there's a factory that was abandoned because it was deemed structurally unsound after a fire. It looks like an old fortress even to people of the Real World. Do you know where it is?"

"I know where everything is in this city," replied Clyde. He swung the car around and Reitrin slammed against the door.

Xitou cursed Clyde's driving as they spun back around, nearly taking out a mailbox, and sped off in the opposite direction.

"It's nearly an hour drive from where we are," said Clyde, "on the other side of the city. Prince, tell Hiro where we're going. We may need backup standing by if it's a trap."

Xitou took a cell phone from his jacket and flipped it open.

"Do we have a way to prepare for what we're heading into?" Reitrin asked nervously.

"Not really," replied Clyde. He was speeding with flashing blue dash lights on. Cars ahead of them pulled over to let them pass. "All we can do is hope they aren't waiting for us. We'll have to park out of sight and walk."

"There isn't much cover out there," Reitrin muttered, trying to recall what the industrial park looked like.

"No, so this is going to be fun," replied Clyde.

"Hiro says he'll have reinforcements waiting nearby," said Xitou, snapping the phone shut. "He wanted me to tell you he's suspected the industrial park was being used by book jumpers for a while now but never had reason to send his men in. He warns us to be cautious and tells Reitrin to be smart or we could all die."

Reitrin felt the pressure crash over her like a wave. The mission was hers. Clyde may have taken over for the drive, but once they got to the factory she would be in charge.

The drive was tense now that she realized the gravity of the situation. She wished she had never taken up Traitor's request.

Reitrin looked out the windshield but felt like she wasn't seeing anything. She was soon gazing at the buildings of the industrial park. They were tall and white and Reitrin gazed up at the tall chimneys.

"A fortress," Xitou muttered.

"These buildings are newer and still in use," Clyde said as he drove slowly down the wide road. There were many large buildings. Some had rounded roofs and large bay doors, but others were taller with more windows or no windows at all. Cars were parked in the lots and Reitrin realized people were working in the buildings.

"We're probably being watched," she said nervously.

"There's no law against us being here," Clyde replied. "However, there are plenty of laws against breaking into an abandoned building." He nodded ahead of them. Reitrin leaned forward to see better.

The abandoned factory was gigantic. It was made of old red brick and wrapped around a smaller building with rusted siding. Its windows were boarded up or busted and Reitrin shivered.

Even from a distance she could sense something was not right. Like the shivers she felt when she faced

Traitor, the building emitted a dark aura that gave her goosebumps. Reitrin wanted to turn back.

Clyde pulled off into one of the empty parking lots near a factory with a green roof. He turned off the engine and turned to look at Xitou and Reitrin. "We are likely under surveillance by the neighboring buildings now. The tags on this car will identify it as affiliated with Hirochi, so they shouldn't give us trouble while we're here."

"But what about when we trespass on that private property?" Reitrin asked, gazing over her shoulder towards the old factory. There was moss growing all around it and a steel fence surrounded it.

"That's up to you. You're the one in charge here. What's our story?"

"You received an anonymous distress call," Reitrin told him, keeping her eyes on the building. "They said they saw suspicious characters loitering out here and we were sent by Hiro to check it out." She looked back at Clyde who held her gaze with a steady look that made her uncomfortable.

"Sounds good." Clyde unbuckled his seat belt and unlocked the car. The three of them stepped out into the warm spring day and Reitrin wrapped her arms around herself. The atmosphere made her shiver.

Clyde opened the back of the car and tossed her a black jacket with the Secret Police emblem on the back. Reitrin caught it and examined it. There was a sword crossing a rifle and a shield in front of them with SP in the center.

"If you're the *Secret* Police, why do you openly wear this emblem?" Reitrin wondered. "Shouldn't you try to be more … secretive?”

“To pedestrians that ask, we are *Security Personnel*,” Clyde answered as he slipped off his cloak, wrapped it up, and tossed it in the trunk. He began to remove his plated armor, piece by piece. Beneath it he wore modern clothing.

“We of the Secret Police work in the shadows,” he explained as he plucked off the plated armor. “We strive to keep book jumpers a secret, but sometimes pedestrians like you get wrapped up in our business and we have to explain away what is happening. Hirochi handles the legal half of this. Maybe it’s because he has endless banks of data in his mind, but he makes every cover story believable and probable. He has even established with the local law enforcement that we are connected to the federal government. If they run our vehicle’s tags we show up as federal troopers and are left alone.”

“Really?” Reitrin tilted her head. “Isn’t that illegal?”

“It would be, if it were a lie,” Clyde replied as he finished removing his armor and slid off his leather tunic and chain-mail over his head. He laid it in the trunk. “If you had over a hundred years to establish and grow an organization, collecting data on the rules and regulations of this world, don’t you think you’d have time to acquire such legal titles and also pay off local law enforcement to look the other way?”

Reitrin gawked at him. “Hiro would do that?”

“He does what he has to in order to protect this world and the people working for him.”

Reitrin shook her head in disbelief. “I can’t believe I’ve never heard of any of this.”

"We're the Secret Police, Ms. Nichol. That's the point. By the way, that jacket is fire resistant." He lifted the lid of a secret compartment in the trunk and withdrew two rifles. One of these he passed to Xitou who examined it sourly.

"I don't like these," he grumbled.

"Proper precautions are necessary, Prince."

Clyde slammed the trunk shut. He slipped the rifle strap around his neck and shoulder before facing Reitrin. Now, he and Xitou both wore rifles and swords, just like the emblem on their jackets.

"Your bodyguards are ready," Clyde said. "What's your first move?"

Reitrin studied the abandoned factory and then looked around the area. She felt as if a thousand eyes were watching her, waiting to ruin any plan she came up with. What if she got them all killed?

"Calm down, Reitrin," Clyde said.

Reitrin jumped at the change in his typically cruel tone. When she looked back at him, he was grinning at her.

"You're not alone in this. We're here to help you."

Reitrin swallowed hard then pulled on the jacket and nodded.

"Can we search outside the fence to try and find a second way in?" she asked as she zipped up the jacket.

"If you wish," replied Clyde. The kindness he had shown melted away as he examined the rusty old fence. There were young trees growing around the area and vines crawling up the fence. The front gate was locked shut with warning signs and a chain that would have to be cut for them to gain entrance.

"Let's start looking then," said Reitrin. She crossed the parking lot with Xitou and Clyde following her.

Their footsteps crunched on dry weeds, gravel, and crushed brick. Reitrin moved away from the fence to walk on the dead grass, but it made little difference in how loud her steps were. She wished she could walk as silent as Etakai at a time like this.

"Look." Xitou pointed ahead of them. "The fence has been cut."

Reitrin and Clyde followed his gaze and saw that the fence was hanging open. They moved forward with caution and examined the opening. It was big enough for them to walk through.

"This wasn't cut open with wire cutters," said Clyde, setting his gloved hand behind the cut fence. "It's melted along the opening."

"Fire?" Reitrin wondered, looking at the wires that were rolled back from the opening.

"I'm sure it was," Clyde said, stepping away. "And the only people in this Real World that use fire in that way are the Eysheus."

"Are you sure?" Reitrin asked.

Clyde nodded. "Most magical beings have trouble using magic in the Real World. I'm sure now that we'll be walking into a trap if we pass through here."

"Not a surprise," said Reitrin as she stood in the opening and looked through. "Traitor just happened to have the time to escape the sight of the Eysheus and ask me for help. It's fishy, but his plea for help sounded real to me."

The ground on the other side was concrete with grass and saplings growing through the cracks. Pieces of rubble were scattered across the concrete and parts of the brick walls had caved in, showing the old rafters and sections of fire damage.

"There's no way to know what they're planning," said Clyde as he slid his rifle into his hands. "Either we go in and risk our lives, or we turn back and abandon the mission."

Reitrin looked back towards the industrial park where she knew the car was parked. She had come this far. It would be embarrassing to turn back, and it could also mean abandoning an innocent woman, if Traitor's story was true.

"I'm going in," she told them. She looked at Xitou, and then at Clyde. "I'm sorry if everything goes wrong."

"It's nothing new," Clyde told her.

Xitou nodded in agreement.

Reitrin stepped through the fence into the large open area beyond.

The towering walls of the factory made her feel minuscule. She looked up at the three-story facade and the broken windows. She breathed out and her breath turned to mist.

"It's cold," said Xitou, his hand on his sword hilt with his rifle hanging forgotten over his shoulder.

"We're in danger," Clyde muttered.

"When Traitor entered my apartment, it got cold," Reitrin said quietly. "He must be nearby."

"It's possible," Clyde said. "But don't stake everything on that. Anything could be in here. Always assume the worst."

There were open garage doors with crumbly concrete ramps leading up to them. Reitrin led the way up the closest ramp and peered inside the factory.

The sunlight shining through holes in the wall provided the only light. Specks of dust floated through the sunbeams and broken rafters cast strange shadows across the rubble on the floor. They had to pick their way through piles of junk inside the large room.

Reitrin wasn't sure what she was looking for. She had a feeling they would know when they were on the right track. Anything that did not fit with the Real World would tip her off and direct them, but as far as she could tell it was nothing more than an old factory.

Were they in the wrong place all together?

"Where does that door lead?"

Reitrin looked around for Xitou, who was across the room in front of a big steel door. It had burns on it, but besides that it looked unharmed.

"It seems like a storage room of some kind," Clyde commented as he and Reitrin picked their way through the rubble to the door. Xitou moved aside to let Reitrin inspect the door.

"I think it's locked," Reitrin said as she checked the latch. She tried to turn it, and it clicked open.

Reitrin whipped around to look at Clyde and Xitou. They were armed and ready, so Reitrin turned back to the door and slowly pulled it open.

The hinges groaned, echoing through the whole factory. Reitrin held her breath as she pulled it open.

Sand began to dump out of the opening.

Reitrin retreated as it spilled quickly into the open space. Clyde and Xitou hurried out of the way with her, but it was Clyde who grabbed her and lifted her off the ground. Reitrin shouted in alarm, but then she saw why he had picked her up.

The sand was moving on its own. It throbbed as if something was beneath it.

The sand growled at the same moment the openings around them were sealed off by light blue barriers.

"Blue energy," Xitou cursed under his breath. "Fevros is here."

"Of course he is," Clyde said, backing away from the sand with Reitrin in his arms.

Sand poured into the room like water as the trio scrambled as far from it as they could. They were at the far wall, unable to do anything but watch as the sand took the form of a towering creature. It had large, drooping eyes, a line across its face, and long sandy arms with disfigured fingers that changed shape as it moved them.

Reitrin wanted to scream, but no sound came from her. The groan of the creature echoed around them, shaking the walls and making chunks of brick and rafters tumble to the ground. Its eyes rolled, searching for the ones who had opened the door.

"What do we do?" Xitou breathed. He was white as a sheet, and so was Reitrin.

Clyde at least looked calm. He set Reitrin down. They could go no further.

When Reitrin glanced down she saw the sand was touching their feet. The grains wrapped around her feet and ankles. This would be the end if she didn't think of something fast.

"Sand drones are weak on the inside," Clyde

whispered.

"How do you know what that is?" Xitou hissed.

"I read the stories inside Hiro's personal library. A hobby I recommend to you both."

Reitrin blinked, but then watched as the drone opened its mouth and nearly fifty rows of long fangs protruded from its throat. It slid towards them on the sand faster than Reitrin had expected.

"They don't play games," she said. She seized Xitou's sword before he could react and ran at the creature.

Xitou yelled at her to stop.

She met it in the middle of the room and jumped towards the fangs.

Reitrin saw the back of the throat was flesh and hurled Xitou's sword just before the fangs closed in around her.

Red fire exploded around them, shattering the fangs and launching Reitrin across the room.

She crashed through the rubble and sand. Reitrin's body ached as she tried to get up, but Clyde appeared beside her and he caught her arm to stop her.

"Don't move yet," he hissed. "Look."

Reitrin blinked as blood trickled between her eyes. She did not wipe it away, though. She was staring at the sand drone. The red flames were devouring it and it was melting, its eyes rolling in rage and pain.

When it was gone, the flames vanished at once.

Reitrin felt Clyde release her, but he remained protectively by her side.

The blue walls of energy were gone, shattered by

the red fire, and the cause was standing in the center of the room.

"Sorry about my messy entrance," said Aoiro as he turned to face Reitrin and Clyde. His blood red hair was speckled with sand and his dark eyes were sharp with annoyance.

Reitrin could not believe her eyes.

Why was Aoiro there?

Chapter Eleven
The Secret Ally

"Fashionably late," Clyde said.

Aoiro dusted sand off the sleeves of his dark red blouse. He wore a vest over it, and black slacks with shiny shoes.

"I try to be fashionable in all aspects of life," Aoiro replied with a smile. It vanished as he glared at Reitrin. "What the hell were you thinking?"

"I told her it was weak on the inside," Clyde retorted sharply. "She came to the same conclusion I did. The only chance we had was tackling it head on and cutting open its throat from the inside."

"Of all the people to go," Aoiro growled, "you two should be the last, and you *know* why that is, Clyde."

Clyde shot to his feet. "The prince was paralyzed, and I was prepared to save her. She was in the clear–"

"The blade was going to miss!"

Aoiro's glare locked on Reitrin who returned it. Aoiro showed up, saved them, and was now yelling at them. Who did he think he was?

"I knew you were the backup Hiro would send," Clyde said. "And I knew you'd save her if the blade went crooked."

"You gambled both your lives," Aoiro snarled. "What if he hadn't sent me?"

"Backup?" Reitrin was on her feet before she knew it and pointing at Aoiro who raised his eyebrows. "But you're the enemy!"

Clyde crossed his arms and looked at Aoiro. "Oh, this is going to be fun. You can take care of the explanation."

"Gee, thanks," said Aoiro with a bitter glare.

"Explain what?" Reitrin was almost screaming. This man had kidnapped her twice, Once in *Blood River*, and then again in *The Lord of Desolation*. He had told her himself that he was a villain. Sure, he had helped her too; giving her the means to rescue Etakai from a poorly written history book, as well as advising her on how to get out of the book. But he claimed that had been for his own reasons too. So how come he was the backup Hiro sent?

Aoiro sighed. He retrieved Xitou's sword from the sand and tossed it to the prince, who caught it by the handle and sheathed it.

"Allow me to be formal," said Aoiro to Reitrin. He swept into a bow and then straightened up with a sheepish smile that did not look quite right on his normally stern face. "My name is Aoiro. I am an Eysheus, an enemy of Fevros, and co-founder of the Secret Police."

"What?" Reitrin felt hollow. Her mind was spinning. "But … all this time …" He had made her think they were enemies, and now he claimed he was an ally?

And co-founder of the Secret Police?

Aoiro rubbed his neck. "I can't just tell you to believe me." He glanced at Clyde. "Help?"

"You should not have chosen this situation for your surprise appearance," said Clyde. He was clearly enjoying Aoiro's suffering. "We need our leader to be focused and now you've ruined any hope of that."

"No."

Clyde glanced at Reitrin with surprise. She was glaring at Aoiro.

"I can focus," she said. "If he's an ally, then you can explain more when the mission is finished. Right?"

"Precisely," replied Aoiro with a grin.

"Then I'll make one thing clear," Reitrin said as she strode up to him, sliding a little on the sand and rubble. He was a head taller than her, but she glared up into his dark eyes. "I don't trust you. So you had better follow my lead. If you make one wrong move I'll figure out some way to end you."

"What if you're ended before I can be ended?" Aoiro mused, rubbing his chin as he looked away from her. The gesture was pure mockery and Reitrin wanted nothing more than to punch him in the face.

"Then Etakai will finish you off," she told him. "I'm sure he'll figure out a way."

"After all he's been through, I would hope so," Aoiro said under his breath.

"Can we move out?" Clyde asked. "We've been immobile too long."

"Right." Reitrin walked away, crossing the room alone.

"Lead the way," Aoiro said with a deep bow.

Clyde smacked the back of Aoiro's head before he followed Reitrin.

Xitou also fell in line and Aoiro trailed after him, still grinning as he rubbed the sore spot on the back of his head.

Down the hallway, they found old office areas

where there were piles of ashes, smashed file cabinets, and crushed desks. A steel rafter had fallen from the top floor, leaving a large hole and collapsed walls that let them see up all four floors. Reitrin saw the pieces of a toilet scattered around one of the rooms.

Reitrin wondered if anyone had been in the factory when it caught on fire? She didn't want to find any skeletons.

They turned down a new corridor and Reitrin paused. Ahead of them was a door with a field of blue energy across it.

"That's promising," Aoiro muttered from the back of the group.

Reitrin ignored him. The door was at the end of the hallway. Reitrin moved to approach it, but both Clyde and Xitou reached to stop her.

"You're familiar with Etakai's energy shields, aren't you?" Xitou asked when Reitrin looked back at him. He was watching the shield with concern. "If you touch it, it could hurt you."

"It might not," Reitrin argued.

"Fevros doesn't do anything with the intent to sting," Aoiro told her. "He always aims to kill, or to manipulate."

Reitrin shot Aoiro a glare over her shoulder.

He met it with a smile. "May I? I'm sure you don't mind me risking my life, right?"

Reitrin glanced at Clyde.

He shrugged. "None of us can do a thing about it."

Reitrin sighed and moved aside so Aoiro could pass her.

The Eysheus approached the door. His black eyes gained a red glow that circled the outside of his irises. Red energy collected in his hand and he slashed it across the blue energy.

A burst of power made the others slide back along the floor.

When they looked up the shield was down. Aoiro glanced at Reitrin, pointed at the doorknob, then at himself.

He wanted to go through first.

Reitrin shook her head.

Aoiro shrugged and backed away from the door.

Reitrin went to the door, set her hand on the doorknob and felt a jolt of cold pain go through her fingers. She blinked, but then pushed the door open.

Sunlight poured down on her and she stepped into a room that was filled with windows, greenery, and a trickling fountain.

The abandoned factory was gone, and when Reitrin looked back she could not find the door she had passed through. She was alone in the round room. There was a table with warm tea and cakes and two chairs, and one was occupied by a familiar man.

"I'm relieved," he said. His black hair was slicked back, and his blue eyes were as bright as ever. His fur coat was draped over the back of his chair and he wore a fine black suit with a white tie. "I was almost certain you'd send one of your guards through the door first."

Reitrin stood motionless. She had met this man in Xitou's storybook world. He had mocked Xitou, avoided answering questions, and then vanished just before when a monster attacked them. He was also the man who had attacked Etakai and blew open the street, destroying her apartment.

His name was one Reitrin would not forget.

"Fevros," she said.

Fevros lifted his teacup to her in greeting. "Please, join me." He motioned to the empty chair.

Reitrin did not move.

Fevros sipped his tea without a care. "So, how is Etakai?" He looked at Reitrin over the teacup.

"He's none of your business," said Reitrin, narrowing her eyes.

"Ah, but I've known him since he was a child," said Fevros with a smirk. "I think he is my business."

"I disagree."

"Are you not angry with him for trying to kill you?"

"You made him turn on us."

"And you magically made him stop," Fevros countered, irritation creeping into his tone. "I am curious about that, so I decided to arrange this meeting. How did you manage to stop his attack?"

"I don't owe you any answers," Reitrin replied.

Fevros held her gaze, then lowered his teacup onto its saucer. "I don't like you, girl." He placed the saucer on the table. "Here I am, being as nice as I can be in this situation, and you're acting like a brat."

"You shouldn't lecture me on actions," Reitrin retorted. "Tell me where I am and I may answer your question."

Fevros watched her carefully. "You are inside a storybook. The characters are away from this home for the next few days, so I planted a little trap on that door to bring the first person to open it into this cozy greenhouse with me."

Reitrin was relieved. If she was just inside a book then that meant she would be able to get out.

"I don't know how I stopped Etakai," she told Fevros as he lifted his teacup to his lips. "I just knew I had to, so I hung onto him and talked to him until he was himself again."

A snap of blue flame from Fevros's eyes made the teacup in his hand shatter. Tea splattered everywhere.

Reitrin jumped, but held her ground when Fevros lowered his hand, the handle of the teacup still in his grasp.

"That's it?" He stared at the broken handle in his fingers, the blue glow of his eyes lingering. Reitrin realized this was not the answer he had wanted to hear. He may have looked calm, but his fingers were trembling with suppressed rage.

"That's it," Reitrin answered. "Now, tell me where Wyvetta is."

Fevros blinked twice and looked up at her with a twisted smile on his face.

Reitrin's stomach plummeted. The menace behind his smile made her knees shake. His calm composure was gone.

Fevros had snapped.

"No," he told her with a laugh. "Oh no, no, no, young lady, you are getting no more answers from me." He whipped out an hourglass from inside his fur coat and slammed it onto the table. The top was half empty with the base filling up fast. There could not have been more than a few minutes left inside.

"Find the prisoner before the sand runs out," he

told her with an ugly smile. "Or you and your companions will be crushed along with her."

Reitrin gave a start and Fevros snapped his fingers. In a burst of light Reitrin found herself back in the factory, stumbling backwards into someone's arms.

She jerked away from the person and heard three voices shout her name in alarm.

"Where did you go?" Xitou asked behind her. In front of her were Clyde and Aoiro, both with worried expressions.

"Fevros has a timer!" Reitrin explained quickly. "He trapped me in some book just then and wanted to know how I stopped Etakai from going crazy. He was unhappy and then pulled out an hourglass and told me to find the prisoner before the time was up."

"This isn't a training mission anymore," said Aoiro to Clyde. "We have to hurry."

"Reitrin, since Fevros is directly involved with this you need to hand the mission over to us," Clyde told her. "Xitou will escort you back to the car and–"

"I'm not leaving," Reitrin snapped. "Not now. That man is the one who has been hurting Etakai and I won't stand for that." She noticed Aoiro shift his weight with an uncomfortable frown. "Aoiro, tell me where Fevros would hide a prisoner."

"In a dark and scary place," replied Aoiro. "But there are quite a few places like that here. It could be almost anywhere."

"We don't have time to search every floor of this building," Reitrin pondered. "And I don't want us to risk splitting up either. Who knows what other kinds of monsters and traps Fevros may have hidden in this place for us?"

"You're learning to think logically," Clyde told her. "Fevros is a storybook character and might lean towards the cliché."

"Cliché would be the windowless metal building out there." Reitrin pointed through a hole in the wall to the metal building. It was tall, the metal siding stained by rust, and there was a chain and lock keeping the door shut.

Inside it would surely be dark and creepy.

Aoiro sighed. "We need to start somewhere, I guess."

"Come on then." Reitrin ran down the hall to the largest hole in the wall that opened into the concrete square. She stumbled over the pile of rubble and ran to the building. It was taller and eerie up close. It sent shivers down her spine as she slowed to a stop before the door.

"How are we going to get in–?" Reitrin jumped when Aoiro and Clyde ran past her and slammed against the door.

The old hinges burst, spitting rust as the door crashed inward.

Two monstrous creatures shot through the door. They had six eyes on their long, greyhound faces and four skinny limbs.

Clyde shouted profanities in his alarm, moving backwards and lifting his rifle.

Reitrin threw herself to the ground when his rifle rattled off rounds.

One of the monsters leapt over her to face Xitou who drew his sword. The other chased Aoiro who was backing away fast, his eyes glowing red with fire.

Reitrin stood up as Clyde ceased firing and turned his focus to helping Xitou. She ran into the shed while the monsters were distracted.

Inside there were tall shelves stocked with boxes. Reitrin paused, leaning her hand on a shelf to catch her breath. Her heart was racing and her breath rattled in her chest. She swallowed hard and pushed herself off the shelf.

The ground within the maze of shelves were visible only by threads of light breaking in through rusted holes in the walls. Looking left and right, Reitrin listened for any sounds that were not coming from the men fighting outside.

She ran down clear paths, slowing to glance around each corner. It seemed there had only been two monsters inside the building. Further back the shelves were replaced by stacks of boxes and pieces of large replacement parts for machinery leaning on the wall.

Reitrin reached the back of the building.

There was a single chair in a dusty sunbeam. A girl was bound hand and foot to the chair. Her chin rested on her chest.

Reitrin ran to the girl. She had long brown hair and a pretty face with tear stains on her cheeks. Reitrin leaned over her and checked if she was breathing.

She was. The girl was alive.

Reitrin began untying the ropes that bound her. She wished she had a knife to cut them.

Once freed, the girl fell forward into Reitrin's arms without waking.

Reitrin seized her around the waist, lifting one of

the girl's arms around her shoulders and hoisted her up. The girl was heavy and Reitrin struggled to hurry as she dragged the girl back through the maze of shelves and out into the open. She had almost forgotten she was on a time limit. How much longer before Fevros's timer ran out?

Xitou had just cut the throat of one of the dogs, which was full of bullets from Clyde's rifle. It fell with a splat into a pool of blood. The other dog was on fire, and no longer moving. Aoiro stood above it with a vengeful glare, but then his eyes snapped to Reitrin.

He and Clyde's jaws dropped at the sight of the girl Reitrin carried.

"That's not Wyvetta," Clyde said. His face was white as a sheet.

"Who is it?" Xitou asked, giving Aoiro and Clyde a puzzled look.

"Her name is Alia," Aoiro explained, trying to regain his composure, but he was failing. "She … she's not supposed to be here. She should still be in her own storybook."

"Then where's Wyvetta?" Reitrin stared at them with fear. "If this isn't her, then what is Fevros going to do to Wyvetta when time runs out?"

"I don't know," Aoiro answered.

The ground began to rumble and the walls of the building crumbled.

A tall chimney crashed to the ground behind the shed. Chunks of rubble flew at Reitrin. She screamed, but a red shield appeared above her. The debris bounced away and smashed the concrete a safe distance away. Reitrin looked at Aoiro and saw the red rings in his eyes were glowing.

"We have to get out of here," said Clyde as the walls collapsed all around them.

"Hurry," said Aoiro, waving the others on. "Go back to your car."

Clyde ran to Reitrin and took Alia from her. Together, they followed Xitou away from the collapsing building.

The front gate had already been broken open. Reitrin wondered if it had been Aoiro, but she had no chance to ask.

Aoiro was no longer with them.

Once they were through the gate Reitrin paused to look back for him, but the man was nowhere to be seen.

"Come on! We can't stop here," Clyde urged.

Reitrin turned away and hurried with him back to the parking lot where the car waited.

She sat in the back with Alia resting against her and Xitou sat upfront.

Clyde started the car and they sped off.

Reitrin looked out the back window at the cloud of dust rising higher and higher into the sky. The factory was reduced to rubble as she watched, and her heart began to sink.

They had not found Wyvetta.

The mission had failed.

Chapter Twelve
The Trap in Her Eyes

Reitrin's eyelids were heavy, but she was unable to rest them. She watched Alia's sleeping face and wondered what had happened to Wyvetta. Would her story be turned to dust if she died in the Real World? There was no way it wouldn't. Reitrin could still remember everything about Traitor, which meant his storybook was just fine, so maybe Wyvetta had not met an untimely end in the collapse. This hope was the only comfort she had.

Clyde drove them back down the secret tunnel they had come through. It was not long before he pulled into his parking spot.

"Keep the jacket," he told Reitrin before he got out of the car.

Reitrin nodded and watched as Clyde opened the door and carefully picked up Alia. His face was pale and he held the woman as if she were made of glass. Something about Alia made the man look ill.

Xitou opened her door, making Reitrin jump and look out at him. He met her gaze and then stood back to let her out.

"You did better leading the mission than I expected," he said.

"Thanks, I had practice in a history book." Reitrin replied as she got out of the car. She didn't feel like talking. After everything that had happened, her mind was too full of questions and her heart heavy with failure.

She walked past Xitou with her head down and followed Clyde back into the busy hideout.

Xitou frowned before catching up with her.

The hallways were still crowded and noisy, but many people stopped to stare at them as they passed by. Most of them were watching Clyde and Alia. A woman in a black dress ran on ahead of them, her high heels clicking loudly.

Xitou remained at Reitrin's side, but she did not pay him any attention. The mission had failed, and Aoiro was missing. Where had he disappeared to? And why did she care?

She slapped her cheeks, trying to focus.

Xitou gave her a worried look.

Soon they were knocking on Hiro's office door.

The door opened and Hiro looked out at them. His golden eyes lingered on Alia and a cold expression crossed his face.

"Put her on the sofa," he said, pushing open the door and standing aside.

Clyde entered and the dinging sound filled the room. Hiro ignored it and waved Xitou and Reitrin inside as Clyde went to the brown sofa at the back of the office. Hiro slammed the door shut but it did not rouse Alia from her unconscious state.

"She must have been drugged," Hiro muttered. He snapped his fingers, making the dinging sound stop. He then joined Clyde beside the sofa. He looked down at the girl then glanced at Clyde. "Will you be okay?"

Clyde nodded and stepped away from the sofa, keeping his eyes on Alia. "I'll stay for the report," he muttered in a weak voice, "but I would like to request leave for a while afterwards."

"After the report, I'll give you the rest of the day off," Hiro told him. "That's the best I can do." He then turned and looked at Reitrin and Xitou. "Time for the details," he said, walking around to the back of his desk and sitting down. He motioned to the seats across from him, which Reitrin accepted, but Xitou remained standing.

"I received Xitou's call about the suspicion of the old factory and I sent backup," said Hiro, "but since then I have heard nothing. Now you all show up with this." He waved to Alia on the couch. "And there is no sign of Wyvetta. So, how did this happen?"

Reitrin glanced up at Xitou who nodded for her to explain. With a deep breath to steady her nerves, Reitrin began her report. When she got to Aoiro's sudden arrival, she cut herself off and stared at Hiro, who frowned as if he had known this moment would come.

"Aoiro helped create the Secret Police?" Reitrin demanded.

"He's in a sensitive situation," Hiro explained calmly. "One that could potentially damage the Real World. Fevros wants him dead, but he will not face Aoiro one-on-one, because he fears he will lose. So, he plays games. You, Reitrin, are caught up in one of his games. So are many of my men. Given the unique state of Fevros's game, Aoiro has had to play the villain in your presence to keep you under the radar, so to speak."

Reitrin was speechless.

"We also wanted Fevros to think Aoiro had fallen from his role as a hero and was acting as a villain in desperate attempts to catch Fevros in his own web."

"What?" Reitrin didn't understand. "Aoiro is a hero? If I had known he was good, I could have used his help."

"And that is why you couldn't know," Hiro replied. "Aoiro is a valuable ally and I cannot risk anyone endangering him. So, you will keep our secret. We cannot let even Etakai know of this. Do you understand me?"

Reitrin held Hiro's gaze, but then nodded.

"Good," said Hiro as he leaned back. "Continue."

Reitrin told the story of the moment she was transported into a book and spoke with Fevros. When she mentioned the villain's name, Hiro's expression sharpened.

Xitou moved as if to interrupt, but one glare from Hiro shut him up.

Finally, the story came to an end and Hiro looked at Clyde. "Were the demon dogs familiar to you?"

"No," he replied. "And even Aoiro said they were a new sight to his eyes before Reitrin emerged with Alia from the shed."

"Do you have anything to add to the story?"

"We killed both dogs. The prince and I had our hands full with one while Aoiro burned the other to death."

"Anything more?"

"No, sir."

"Then you're dismissed." Hiro waved Clyde towards the door. "I thank you for your time. I'm sorry this day took an unexpected turn for you."

Clyde saluted and then left the office.

The door clicked shut behind him and Hiro turned to Reitrin. "How do you feel?"

Reitrin was surprised by his question. "I'm–" She wanted to say she was fine, but she knew she wasn't, and she could see in his eyes that Hiro knew it as well.

"I hope you learned something from this," Hiro said. "Being a hero is not easy, but you seem to be up to the challenge. Xitou might be right, and you are possibly not a lost cause as I suspected. With proper mentoring you could be of great use."

Reitrin clasped her hands and watched the floor. "Sir, I failed. I was supposed to find Wyvetta."

"We can't be sure Wyvetta was even there," said Hiro as he stood up.

Reitrin gave a start. "What do you mean?"

"Like I said, Fevros plays games," replied Hiro as he went to the sofa and looked down at Alia. "It's likely Wyvetta was never there, and he meant for you to find Alia all along."

"Why would he do that?"

"We never understand his games until their purpose is fulfilled."

"Sir," said Reitrin carefully. "I might be mistaken, but I think Etakai mentioned a girl named Alia from his world. Is this her?"

"Yes." Hiro looked back at Reitrin. "This is the woman Etakai loves."

Reitrin stared at Alia, her heart sinking. She was confused why this news made her feel so ill. All she could say was, "Oh."

"We need to wake her," said Hiro to Xitou. "Guard the door and if she proves to be lethal, make sure she does not leave this room."

Xitou nodded. He drew his sword and stood in front of the door.

Reitrin watched as Hiro knelt beside the sofa and set his hand over Alia's closed eyes.

A glow of golden light pulsed through Hiro's body, following his blood veins and illuminating the woman's face. Hiro removed his hand and shook it out as if it hurt.

Alia winced and wrinkled her nose, but then opened her clover green eyes. She blinked a few times before examining the room. "Where am I?"

"Don't answer any of her questions," Hiro warned Reitrin and Xitou.

Alia sat up and looked at Reitrin who held her gaze. "Who are you?"

Reitrin remained silent. She could see why Hiro was being so cautious. The girl's eyes were wide as if she were scared. She leaned forward, tilting her head and searching the room with no expression. It looked as if invisible strings were controlling her like a marionette.

"Fevros," said Hiro to the girl. "Let Alia go. You'll get no information out of us."

"Oh, you'll have to kill Alia to make me leave," said the girl with a twisted smile that did not suit her kind features. Alia's eyes widened, alarmed at the words coming from her.

Reitrin clenched her fists. Was Alia aware she was being controlled?

"Remember how this looks," Hiro said over his shoulder. "Only Fevros can control storybook characters against their will, and they have to be unconscious for it to happen."

Reitrin held her breath. She had never heard of such a thing being possible.

"Get out of her," said Hiro again. "I will not warn you again."

Fevros began to laugh through Alia. "I see your office is quite small and wooden. Are you hiding in a cabin in the woods? That would not surprise me. Here I suspected you would have a large facility hidden somewhere out of sight."

Hiro stood up, lifted his hand, and then pointed at Alia's nose.

"Don't come back," he said.

Golden light exploded.

Reitrin crossed her arms over her eyes. When the light faded, she rubbed her eyes and stared at Hiro's back.

Alia lay collapsed on the sofa, holding her hands over her eyes. Her mouth hung open in a silent scream.

Hiro leaned over her and removed her hands from her eyes.

"Tell me your name," he said gently.

The girl stared up at him. "Alia," she whispered back. "I don't know where I am." She looked past him, her gaze scanning everything in the room. She wrapped her arms around herself as if she were cold and then looked back up at Hiro. "Do you work for Fevros?"

Hiro shook his head. "You are in a safe place, but we will need to blindfold you until we can be sure Fevros has left your eyes."

"Left my eyes?" Alia looked frightened. "Am I

still in danger?"

"It's possible," Hiro told her. "So, Alia, do you mind if I blindfold you?"

Alia hesitated, then shook her head, but she was staring at Reitrin now. She looked confused and Reitrin frowned.

"You look familiar," Alia told her.

Reitrin raised an eyebrow and looked at Hiro who met her eye and shook his head. Reitrin remained silent.

Hiro reached back into his desk, pulled out a blindfold, and handed it to Alia. "I will personally escort you to a holding cell," he told her. He turned to Reitrin and Xitou. "You two stay here until I return."

Hiro left with Alia and the door snapped shut behind them.

Xitou heaved a sigh and sank into the empty chair by Reitrin. "You may not realize it, but you did a good job today."

Reitrin shook her head. "I don't think so. Clyde was helping me the whole time."

"It's in his nature to lead," Xitou replied. "But he did let you make the choices."

Reitrin stood up and began to pace. She didn't want to discuss the mission. All she wanted was to leave so she could check on Sia and Etakai. She had left them alone all day. It would be past evening when she returned to the hotel, if not later.

A knock sounded on the door and the two looked up.

The door opened, and the dinging sound filled the room.

"Blast that alarm," said Aoiro as he entered the

room and shut the door behind him. He heaved a sigh and leaned back on the door, his tired gaze looking first at Xitou and then at Reitrin.

"Shouldn't you be getting home?" Aoiro asked.

"I want to," Reitrin said, watching him suspiciously. "Hiro told us to stay here."

Aoiro noted her glare and sighed again. He dislodged himself from the door and crossed the room to drop into Hiro's empty chair. A cloud of brick dust rose from his clothes.

"I hoped Hiro would tell you I am not a danger," he said to Reitrin's glare. "I really am as safe as any other officer in this place."

"We're all dangerous," Xitou told Aoiro.

"I won't harm her." Aoiro gave Xitou a bitter look.

"Why does no one here seem to like Xitou?" Reitrin asked. "Has he insulted you all or something?"

"Nothing like that," replied Aoiro, crossing his arms on the desk and laying his head on them. "Xitou is merely another temporary member of the Secret Police who knows too much, but also too little."

"I'm sitting right here." Xitou crossed his arms.

Aoiro glanced at him, then looked up at Reitrin. "If you'll let me, I'd like to escort you home."

Reitrin narrowed her eyes.

"Hiro and I discussed this earlier," Aoiro told her. "It's risky for me to take you to your hotel, but it would give you a chance to question me all you want about anything, including your father and his whereabouts. Since I'm sure you'd prefer to ask your questions without an audience to voice unnecessary opinions?" He nodded to Xitou who scowled.

Reitrin's heart leapt. "Is my father okay?"

"I'll tell you in the car," said Aoiro as he stood up.

Reitrin looked at Xitou. "I can trust him, right?"

"If he were untrustworthy, he wouldn't be able to get into Hiro's office," Xitou replied. "This place is impossible to break into."

Reitrin sighed, then faced Aoiro. "Okay, I'll go with you."

"Good," said Aoiro with a smile. "Prince, stay here. Hiro will need to speak to you before you're relieved for the day."

Xitou nodded once and looked at Reitrin.

She frowned at him, not knowing what to say. She settled for, "I'll see you later."

"Be vigilant," Xitou replied.

Aoiro went to the door, glancing once at the ceiling that was still dinging loudly, and then pushed open the door.

"Ladies first," he said, motioning for Reitrin to go through.

Reitrin gave him a cold look before leaving the office.

"Will you answer anything before we're in the car?" she asked as they passed through the large room of computers and back through the main hallway.

"I could answer that," Aoiro said as if speaking to himself. "But we're not in the car yet."

Chapter Thirteen
Pestering Aoiro

Aoiro opened the passenger door of Hiro's sedan for Reitrin then went to the driver's side.

"Truthfully," he said as he got in and shut the door. "I was terrified to learn to drive when I first came to the Real World. Hiro insisted that if I were to spend any time here, I would need to learn. Now, I find these cars quite convenient, and I always try to drive Hiro's, since he loves this car and me driving it irks him." He was smiling as he started the engine and backed out of the parking lot.

Reitrin tried hard not to stare at him as he turned the car around and headed up to the gate. The guards did not stop him or question him. They let the gate open, and he drove by, waving to them and receiving salutes in reply.

"You really are a part of the Secret Police, aren't you?" Reitrin wondered.

"Yes," said Aoiro as they drove up the slope to the exit. He pulled a pair of sunglasses out of the glove compartment and slipped them on just before the large doors opened and they drove out into the orange glare of sunset.

"You aren't acting like yourself," Reitrin noticed.

"Correction," said Aoiro, pointing at her nose. "I *am* acting like myself. You met me when I was acting like a villain, so you've not seen me as myself."

"So why did you kidnap my father?" Reitrin shielded her eyes as she looked at Aoiro. It was difficult to believe it was really he that drove the car. The events of the day stretched everything Reitrin had once believed about the Real World.

"I hoped you would figure that out yourself," Aoiro told her. "Take *Blood River* for example. I had no idea you were in that book until I saw you. I knew you were not safe in that story, so I kidnapped you and had Hiro guard you."

Reitrin gawked at Aoiro. "You kidnapped me to protect me?"

"And to test Etakai," replied Aoiro. "When I saw him in the book, I knew things were getting serious for Fevros."

"Why is that?" Reitrin asked.

Aoiro shook his head. "We know too little about Etakai right now to tell you anything for sure. But he seems to trust you. You're the only reason he's still alive. Hiro was going to kill him when you ran out to save him."

Reitrin frowned at the city through the windshield as it sped closer. "Why did you want me to save him from the history book?"

"I have my reasons," Aoiro replied in a dangerous tone. "Now, shall I finish answering your question about your father?"

"Please," replied Reitrin, though she thought she was beginning to understand.

"I took him because he knows too much and could put a lot of us in danger. Including you."

Reitrin stared at him.

That wasn't what she had expected.

"He is being kept safe with the Secret Police, but we don't think you should meet with him until we know for sure that Fevros has not bribed him somehow."

"Fevros was in contact with him?" Reitrin whispered.

"Your father, Harold Nichol, knew a lot more than he should have," Aoiro explained. "I can't tell you more than that right now."

"Why not?"

"You're not ready."

Reitrin scowled. "So you took him as soon as you left *Blood River*?"

"Yes," replied Aoiro. "I had Hiro take him and once he was safe, I removed you and the others. I must say it was hard to convince Hiro he needed his men to report to the library in answer to your distress call. He was already busy. We had to act fast to interrupt your call and then send our own response team. The doctor you met was also one of ours, though he was also hard to convince to help. Not many members of the Secret Police like Etakai."

"Why?" Reitrin asked. The amount of information was making her head hurt. How could the Secret Police have such ties in the city? "Didn't you remove Etakai from his storybook?"

"Yes," replied Aoiro. "For the sake of my future he had to be removed. I just didn't realize he would ever cross paths with you. Fate is a funny thing."

"I don't get it." Reitrin pressed her fingers to her forehead. "What does fate have to do with any of this?"

"Sorry, but you'll have to stay confused until we have more information," Aoiro told her. "I may have already said too much."

"I have more questions than I did before," said Reitrin, rubbing her face. "What do I or Etakai have to do with Fevros and you wanting to kill each other?"

"I don't want to kill him," Aoiro corrected. "He wants me dead, but I just want to send him back to his story where he belongs."

Reitrin looked at Aoiro, who was watching the road with a scowl.

"How did he get out?" she asked.

Aoiro cleared his throat and was silent for a long time. He eventually sighed, then chuckled. "You're too curious, Rei. I wish I could tell you everything, but I really can't. It would put you in danger because you would try to right the wrongs that have been done."

"And why would that be bad?" Reitrin demanded. They were pulling into the hotel parking lot now. "Can't I have a choice on if I want to do anything about this or not?"

Aoiro parked the car and slid off his sunglasses to look at her.

"You are like me," he told her. The gravity in his voice made Reitrin fall silent. "I can't sit by and let people fight a battle I could help in. You would choose to fight, and I cannot risk you being put in more danger than I or any member of the Secret Police can save you from."

"But why do I even matter to you?" Reitrin asked.

Aoiro shook his head. "That's another question I won't answer. Just watch your back. The events of today have put into motion things that could drastically change your situation. You may not have been safe before, but you're certainly not now."

Reitrin held his gaze and then shrugged her shoulders. "I'll figure it out myself then. Whatever I am to you and everything that's going on, I'll find the answers."

Aoiro smirked at her. "Good luck. I don't think anyone knows all the answers though." He waved her to the door. "Get out of here before someone thinks we're suspicious."

"But we are," Reitrin grumbled as she opened her door. She got out of the car and looked back at Aoiro. "Can I tell Etakai about you?"

Aoiro considered her question, but then shrugged his shoulders. "If you think he'll believe you. But he's fought me and been embarrassed by me too often for him to willingly believe I'm a good guy. Not only that, but he may yet be my enemy."

Reitrin gave him a puzzled look.

"Bye, bye," said Aoiro, waving at her.

Reitrin rolled her eyes and shut the door.

Aoiro drove away and Reitrin watched the black sedan as it rounded the bend and left the parking lot.

Chapter Fourteen
Stories

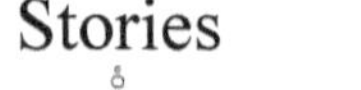

Sia was asleep when Reitrin entered the bedroom. Her sister's arm was bandaged, and she appeared to have been in bed most of the evening. Etakai was motionless as he lay on his back in the second bed. The ceiling fan spun slowly above him and Reitrin went over and sat on the edge of his bed.

"You've been gone a long time," Etakai murmured.

Reitrin rubbed her face tiredly. "Yeah."

"You smell like concrete and dirt." Etakai opened his eyes to look at her. "And you are covered in dust."

"I should shower," Reitrin said, looking across the room to the window. "I went through a lot today, Etakai, and I'm exhausted."

"Typical for dealing with storybook drama," Etakai replied. He shifted his position, but then winced with a sharp intake of breath.

"Don't move around so much," Reitrin said, staring at the bandages around his chest with alarm. She thought she had seen blood seeping through, but it was just the red reflection of the sunset.

"I'm fine," Etakai grumbled. He pushed his pillows under his back so he was sitting up a little and crossed his arms, though this also made him wince and then lower them back to his sides.

"I could use a story to take my mind off my pain," he told her. "And maybe a pain killer." He pouted and looked away from her.

Reitrin sighed and left the bed to fetch his medicine from the bathroom. Etakai hated the pills of the Real World and did not trust them, so he must have been feeling serious pain to be asking for them.

When Reitrin returned she found Sia was sitting up and rubbing the sleep from her eyes.

"You're back," she said, watching Reitrin who went to sit beside Etakai. "How did it go?"

Reitrin frowned, but then shrugged.

"Not a good sign," Etakai commented as Reitrin handed him a glass of water with his pill. "Did you screw up?"

"I think I did," Reitrin muttered as she pulled her legs up onto the bed and held them to her chest. "We never found Wyvetta, but we found someone else." She looked at Etakai. The concern in her eyes must have been an open book to him because after he swallowed the pill, he gave her a sour look.

"Someone I know?" he guessed.

Reitrin nodded and looked at the ground. She was having a hard time believing Alia was someone Etakai would fall for. She was pretty, but Reitrin had expected Etakai to be drawn to someone with more of a heroine's presence.

"What happened to Wyvetta?" Sia asked, wrapping her blanket around herself and crossing her legs. "And Traitor? Did he ever show up again?"

Reitrin shook her head. "I guess I should start from the beginning." She glanced at Etakai who held her gaze. "You probably won't believe a lot of it."

"I'm having trouble just believing you had a fun adventure without me," Etakai retorted. "What more is there left to hear?"

Reitrin rubbed her legs, knocking crumbs of sand and dirt off her jeans. "It started when I was on my way to the library this morning," she began, watching the floor so as not to see Etakai and Sia's reactions. "Hiro and Xitou were trailing me, and Hiro kept saying I wasn't impressive." She fell into the story, feeling tired as she relived it all in her mind. She was surprised that Etakai did not interrupt. He folded his hands across his abdomen and watched the ceiling.

Reitrin told them about Hiro assigning Xitou and Clyde as her bodyguards and Etakai snorted.

"Clyde," he muttered, making Sia and Reitrin look at him. He was glaring at the ceiling.

"Hiro said he was from your story," Reitrin said.

Etakai nodded. "He almost killed me." He lifted his hand and placed it over a white scar across his collarbone. "I was helping Alia get out of the castle and Clyde caught us. We fought, and I was cocky so I didn't think he would get me. But he did." Etakai lowered his hand and shut his eyes. "But I'm not the one telling the story, so I'll wait."

"No, tell us," said Reitrin. She wanted to know more about the man she had traveled with. "What happened? Why were you two enemies?"

Etakai shook his head. "We weren't always enemies. When we were little, we trained together and became good friends. Both of our fathers were a part of the royal guard. Mine was Captain of the King's Navy, his was a Captain of the Guard."

"Your father was a sailor?" Reitrin asked.

Etakai nodded and a look of pride crossed his face as he gazed at the ceiling. "Captain Etakai

Fasentario. The greatest sea captain ever known."

Sia and Reitrin exchanged looks of surprise.

"You never told us you were named after your father," Reitrin said.

"I don't recall telling you anything about me," Etakai retorted. "I don't use my last name anyway. It would tie me to him, since he was so highly respected that only his closest friends knew his first name. But he wasn't my blood father. He found me adrift in the ocean …" Etakai faded to silence.

Reitrin waited, but he did not continue. She sighed, and explained how Clyde took over the start of the mission. When Reitrin said Clyde had been a part of the Secret Police for a long time it made Etakai look at her again, but he did not interrupt.

She told them about the industrial park and how Clyde had given her the jacket she still wore. Sia made a comment about it being a nice jacket, but that was the only interruption before Reitrin told them about the sand drone.

Here, Reitrin cut herself off and set her hand over her mouth.

Etakai and Sia waited, but Reitrin's heart was racing.

How would Etakai react to Aoiro's role in the rescue?

"What was it?" Sia asked anxiously. "Did it hurt you? Are you in need of medical attention?"

"She's clearly intact," Etakai snapped.

Sia hunched her shoulders.

"Well," Reitrin continued. "Clyde said its weakness was in the back of its throat, so I took Xitou's sword and charged it."

"Who saved you?" Etakai's direct question made Reitrin stare at him.

"It was Aoiro."

Etakai jolted forward, then fell back into the pillows, cursing.

Sia covered her mouth with her hands.

"I was suspicious of him," Reitrin explained before Etakai could blow up at her. "But he was helpful, and … funny. He told me he acted as my enemy to keep me safe from Fevros."

Etakai was breathing hard, but he was cringing and held his hand over his chest. "You trust him?"

Reitrin held Etakai's gaze. "No. I don't trust him. He says you may still be his enemy, whatever that means. But he is a founder of the Secret Police, same as Hiro."

"Then they're all fools," Etakai shot.

Reitrin drew back with a pained look. "Etakai," she tried to speak, but Etakai threw back the blanket and stood up.

"Hey!" Sia cried when Etakai struggled to walk to the door.

"Etakai, don't." Reitrin jumped up and barred the door with her arms out wide.

Etakai faced her, his eyes glowing. "Move. I want no part of the Secret Police if they're working with two of my enemies. Anyone who trusts Clyde or an Eysheus is a moron I don't need in my life."

Reitrin was speechless. "Are you serious?" She lowered her arms. She was too hurt by his words to believe them. "You'll stop being my friend because I worked with them on one mission?"

"Yes."

The two of them held each other's gaze. Then they heard a knock on the front door.

"I'll get it." Sia slipped past Reitrin and squeezed out the door behind her, then shut it.

Etakai scoffed and looked away.

Reitrin narrowed her eyes sadly. "I guess I was asking for this. I could have kept it secret, in fact he suggested I do, but I wanted you to know. I wanted to be able to talk to you about it. If I had known you would react this way, I would have never told you."

Etakai scowled, but then looked at the door behind her. He grabbed her and threw them both to the ground seconds before the door burst open with a loud crash.

Sia screamed.

A demon creature hung over them, holding Sia in a hand with thin fingers and long claws. Its huge body was like a long black snail.

The monster's head was long with a large gaping mouth. Its fangs were dripping with saliva and it was panting. The creature lifted the arm that held the screaming Sia and rubbed its empty eye sockets. It was then Etakai and Reitrin noticed the dark blood oozing from its face.

Someone had recently gouged out its eyes.

Etakai held his hand over Reitrin's mouth to keep her silent. The monster slithered into the room, circling the wall and tapping the floor and beds, searching for them. It could not see them and did not know their scent, but it would surely hear them, as it could hear Sia screaming every time it moved its arms.

They were both unarmed and the monster filled

the whole room with its long body. It stood on its free hand and trembled as if excited for when it found the other humans. It sniffed Sia, making her wail in terror again. She was staring at Etakai and Reitrin, her eyes swimming with tears, begging them to save her.

But how were they going to do that?

The creature lowered its hand, but then hissed as it turned its head back through the doorway. A black glow came from the other room and the creature slithered away and let the next person enter.

It was Traitor. His hood hid him, and his bow was notched with a black shafted arrow.

"I was sent to retrieve you," Traitor told them in his angelic voice. "Resist and you die."

Chapter Fifteen
The Pawn of Fevros

Reitrin stared at Traitor speechlessly. He truly was a traitor. After all she had gone through in hopes of saving Wyvetta, he now turned on them as if none of it had even happened. However, Reitrin could not scold him because Etakai's bandaged hand was still covering her mouth.

"You two look cozy," Traitor told them. "Fated lovers?"

"Shut your shadowy face," Etakai growled in an icy voice. "I was about to walk out of this hotel when you showed up with your demon."

"It is no more demon than I," Traitor said. "The only way to tame it was to pull out its eyes."

"Congratulations," Etakai replied.

Reitrin pulled Etakai's hand from her mouth. "How did you get in here undetected?" She was waiting for members of the Secret Police to break down the door and rescue them. She was surprised they hadn't come yet.

"I never left the building," Traitor answered. "This monster and I have remained hidden in this hotel since before your stay."

Reitrin stared in disbelief. "One minute you're begging for help, and now you're threatening our lives."

Traitor stiffened. "I cannot ..." He glanced back at the monster that growled in a high-pitched tone. Traitor's hand tightened on his bow. "I cannot disobey Fevros," he whispered, turning back to Etakai and Reitrin. "He made that trap and forced me to play the part I did. Wyvetta is still in his clutches. I only want to save her–"

The monster screamed with a sound like a fork scraping a glass plate. It lunged at Traitor. He fired the arrow into its mouth, but the monster did not react. It was upon him when Etakai jumped up, blue eye blazing, and threw himself at them.

With a sickening splat, the monster struck a blue shield. It dropped Sia, who landed safely on her bed, though she was shaky and pale.

Etakai drew back his hands when the monster shook its head and shrieked angrily.

Traitor fired five arrows, one after the other, so fast even Etakai was impressed.

The arrows struck the monster's face and it screamed.

"So much for it obeying to you," Etakai said.

"Don't let it get out," Traitor yelled as he ran to the window. "It could eat everyone in this city before dawn."

Etakai kicked the door shut, his blue eye flaming with light. He held up his hands and a huge blue shield wrapped around the monster. It screamed and pounded on the blue energy, only to jerk away in pain. The bubble of blue energy muffled its cries.

"Is it safe to kill?" Etakai called to Traitor who made sure the windows were shut.

"No," replied Traitor. "It has a role in my story. If you kill it my book will die. Can't you heroes do something with it?"

"Sia," Reitrin yelled to her sister. "Toss me that

book you've been reading."

Sia, still in a daze, groped for the book on the bedside table and hurled it past the blue bubble to Reitrin who caught it, opened it, and set her hands on the page.

"I don't know what I'm doing," Reitrin yelled to Etakai and the others. "Just hold on."

She faced the monster that had rounded towards her and was clawing at the bubble so desperately its fingers were bleeding.

"For now," Reitrin told the creature. "You will stay in this book. Stranded on the smallest island the writer could have imagined, far from the story line and out of sight of all characters." She lifted her hand, and then a golden light spilled from the book.

A burst of white light and black letters flew around the room. Reitrin kept her eyes open as the force of magic whipped around her like a strong wind. She gritted her teeth, feeling as if her strength was being sucked into the book with the blue bubble.

She slammed the book shut as soon as the monster was inside.

Everyone else remained.

Reitrin crashed to her knees, holding the book and staring in disbelief. It had actually worked.

"It's a story about submarines," she said, looking up at Etakai and Traitor.

Sia fainted behind them.

"I don't know if I did the right thing," said Reitrin. "But I bought us some time."

"Time to do what exactly?" Etakai inquired. He did not look pleased.

"Find Wyvetta and free Traitor from Fevros's

control," Reitrin explained as she stood up. She glanced at Traitor who unstrung his bow and slipped it into a strap on his quiver.

"I appreciate this," he told her. "If you come with me, I know where she's being kept. It won't be easy to save her, but I think with you two it may actually be possible."

"This is foolish," said Etakai.

"I don't want to trust him again," said Reitrin. "But after all I've gone through today, I'd love to strike a blow to Fevros."

Etakai had to suppress a grin.

"Should I swear on my life that I will not double cross you this time?" Traitor asked.

"You don't look like you have one to swear on," Etakai told him. "What are you, a ghost?"

"Sort of," Traitor answered.

"Well, Miss Hero," said Etakai, turning to Reitrin. "I don't like this one bit, so whatever danger you're planning to run to, I'm going with you. And no, you won't talk me out of it."

Reitrin clenched her jaw, then faced Traitor. "I'll help you if you promise to go into the custody of the Secret Police when we find Wyvetta."

"Why would you ask this?" Traitor wondered.

"They'll keep you safe," Reitrin explained. "They work to keep book jumpers like you out of trouble. They may be able to help you and Wyvetta get home too."

"Then I promise," Traitor replied.

"Good," Reitrin replied. "You'd better keep that promise."

"I will."

"Okay then," said Etakai to Reitrin. "Put your sister to bed properly and pack some pain killers. I'm not going without those."

"You like them now?" Reitrin asked.

"I just fought a monster when I couldn't get out of bed earlier," Etakai replied. "I think for now I'll learn to deal with them."

Chapter Sixteen
Reitrin's Second Chance

The sun had set and fog was settling over the city. Reitrin made her unconscious sister more comfortable on the bed and let Etakai take only one more painkiller before packing two. She didn't want him to take too many.

"Why didn't any of the Secret Police show up to help us?" Reitrin whispered as she and Etakai followed Traitor down the street.

"Shouldn't you know?" Etakai grumbled. "Since you're such great pals with them."

Reitrin pouted at him. "I didn't think you were this petty."

Etakai stuck his tongue out at her, but they stopped talking when Traitor moved into the shadows of the nearest building. Reitrin and Etakai followed and pressed their backs against the cold brick.

They watched silently as something moved across the street. The roads were empty and the traffic light down the street changed from red to green. Beyond the light a strange creature with no head, long limbs, and a transparent body walked slowly across the street and disappeared on the other side of the road.

Reitrin grabbed the sleeve of Etakai's jacket. "It's one of those creatures from Xitou's land," she breathed in his ear. "The creature that climbed the cliff."

Etakai nodded his understanding, but didn't risk

speaking. Where there was one monster on guard, more were surely lurking nearby.

Traitor seemed to be thinking this too. He backed up until he was beside Etakai.

"No more speaking," he warned. "The building he's in is two more blocks away. Stay close behind me."

Etakai and Reitrin nodded.

They sneaked through the alleys, turning this way and that. Traitor would glance around each corner, his bow readied with an arrow.

Reitrin was unfamiliar with this side of the town. She recognized it seconds before they came to a stop at the end of the last alley and saw the old cathedral.

Its bell towers rose high into the dark night and the stones looked damp, almost as if they were bleeding.

Reitrin knew this cathedral. She had walked by it on her way to school when she was a child and always thought it was frightening. It had a sign hanging off the front doors, explaining that it was closed due to fire damage. Nothing had been done to reopen it, and rumors about suspicious causes for its closing were all Reitrin had heard.

Now that she knew what was going on, she wondered if Fevros was behind the cathedral being closed and condemned in the first place.

Traitor looked up and down the street before backing up to stand with Reitrin and Etakai.

"Once inside we'll be vulnerable," he whispered. "Members of the Secret Police cannot get inside this building. Fevros has a magical barrier around it that is invisible and dangerous. As long as you two are with me you should be okay, but your stalking guards will not be able to pass through after us."

"You think we're being followed?" Reitrin whispered.

"I have seen the followers twice now," Traitor whispered back. "Are you ready for this? We may die once we set foot in there. Fevros plays games, but if he senses danger in his domain, he wastes no time terminating it."

"I've been a step away from death for a while now," Etakai muttered, eyeing the cathedral. "Taking another step closer is fine with me."

Reitrin gave him a grim look before nodding to Traitor.

They crossed the street to the cathedral. Before they reached the other side, three creatures dropped from the buildings and landed on the ground in front of them.

Reitrin skidded to a stop and gasped.

The creatures looked human, but their bodies were deformed with animal parts. One of them had the head of a hawk and long feathers growing out of its thin arms, on which he had talons and only three fingers. The other two had faces that were half wolf and tufts of fur on their bodies. There were yellow claws on their hands

"Threats," Traitor whispered.

"They don't look tough," said Etakai, drawing three knives.

"You don't understand," Traitor hissed, backing up when the Threats moved closer. "Fevros only keeps creatures important to their stories near this place. If we kill any of them their stories will turn to dust."

"Ah," muttered Etakai. "That's problematic."

One of the wolf Threats howled and charged.

Etakai's blue shield slammed into them and with a swipe of his hand he locked all three in a blue cage. The creatures howled and screeched. They clawed at the bubble angrily.

"Come on," Etakai barked at Traitor and Reitrin's dumbfounded stares. "If we can't kill them, what are you waiting for?"

"More," replied Traitor, hurrying after Etakai.

Reitrin stared at the Threats. She saw the hawk looking at her. Its head twitched each time it moved.

"Move," Etakai appeared beside her and grabbed her arm. "This is your mission, right? Start leading."

Reitrin glared at him. She shook off his hand and ran to the cathedral. Traitor and Etakai fell in pace behind her.

More Threats leapt off the cathedral and ran at them. Etakai's blue magic blazed across the dark streets, creating a wall that kept the Threats back and led the trio straight to the cathedral door.

"Once inside we'll have no time to waste," Traitor said as he ran. "By now Fevros will know I'm helping you and he could cause Wyvetta pain to try to make me behave."

"If you attack us, I'll kill you," Etakai said, but he was looking pale.

The cathedral door was locked. Etakai cursed as the three of them came to the door. He lifted his hand, releasing the Threats, which charged at them. With a wave, Etakai made the shield wrap around the three of them and the door. The Threats rammed the shield.

Etakai dropped to his knees, his blue eye narrowing as he grew weak.

"Are you okay?" Reitrin turned to him as Traitor worked to unlock the doors.

"I'm fine," Etakai said. His hands shook and the shield wavered. The Threats claws were managing to break through. Etakai saw the claws and forced more energy into the barrier. The Threats were pushed back out as the barrier was revived.

"That doesn't look fine," Reitrin argued.

"We're in." Traitor pushed open the doors.

Reitrin seized Etakai's arm and pulled him into the cathedral. She and Traitor pushed shut the doors and Traitor re-locked them.

The silence inside the cathedral was thick. Nothing moved. The decor was medieval gothic. A dusty chandelier hung over their heads. The stone floor, wooden pews and candelabras were covered in dust and cobwebs. They stood in the narthex. Before them were two large wooden doors of the nave. The wood was cracked from age, but the doorknobs were clean. Footprints in the dust showed the room on the other side was visited frequently.

Reitrin stood over Etakai, who was panting as he held his hand over his blue eye.

"Etakai," said Traitor, looking down at him. "Get up, we have to move."

Etakai hoisted himself up. Reitrin offered her hand. Etakai knocked it away. He was trembling and his eyes were cloudy.

"Etakai," Reitrin whispered with concern.

"This way." Traitor led them down a hallway to their left.

Reitrin didn't want to go. Seeing Etakai in this critical state was frightening.

Etakai followed Traitor and Reitrin stayed near him.

Their footsteps were muffled by the dust in the hallway. There were old plaques on the walls of bishops that had preached in the pulpit and lights hanging every few feet along the ceiling.

Ahead of them there was a stream of light from an open doorway. Traitor stopped when they came to the light. He sidled along the wall and peeked inside. For a moment he was motionless, but then he stood back with Reitrin and Etakai.

"The kitchen," he whispered to them. "Get water for your friend. I'll guard him."

Reitrin nodded and left Etakai's side. He was too weak to argue and as soon as Reitrin left him he sank to his knees.

The kitchen was deserted. A long table was laid out before her with dirty dishes. There were clean dishes drying on the counter beside the large double sink. Reitrin crossed the room to the sink. She found a glass cup among the drying dishes.

She took it and dried it on her shirt then turned the squeaky faucet. The noise made her wince. She filled the glass halfway and then turned off the water. When she turned around, she caught her breath.

A boy stood watching her. His hair was black, his clothes were casual, and his eyes were deep violet.

Reitrin cursed herself. She had not seen him over the pile of dirty dishes.

"You messed up," said the boy.

"I believe you're right," said Reitrin. She looked

towards the doorway and wondered if Etakai and Traitor were okay.

"The guards left a minute ago," the boy said. "Fevros doesn't realize how lazy his men are."

"Are you going to kill me?" Reitrin asked.

The boy rolled his eyes to the ceiling. "No. I'm supposed to bring intruders to Fevros."

"I guess that means I have to fight you."

"It seems that way."

They watched each other for a moment, but neither moved.

"Kind of lame to get caught because you were thirsty," said the boy.

"It's for my–" Reitrin cut off. Did the boy know Traitor and Etakai were outside the door? "It's my first time trying to be a hero," Reitrin said instead. "I'm not surprised I didn't last long."

The boy snorted. "You're a terrible liar."

"And you're a terrible guard."

The boy shrugged. He stepped forward and took the glass from her. "I'm Raith." He offered his hand. "I'll help you get where you need to go."

Reitrin gawked at him. "I can't trust you." She took back the glass instead of shaking hands.

"You're not a complete idiot then," Raith said as Reitrin backed towards the door. "Not turning your back on me would be smart if there weren't someone behind you."

Reitrin spun around, but there was no one there.

Raith started to laugh and Reitrin rounded on him with a glare.

"Geeze," Raith said, wiping a tear from his eye. "You're a terrible hero."

"Why are you messing with me?" Reitrin demanded. "Either take me to Fevros or leave me alone."

The boy heaved a sigh. "Go." He waved her to the door. "I never saw you."

Reitrin stared at him. "This is another trick."

"I heard Traitor and you in the hallway," Raith told her. "You need to give that water to your friend. I'm letting you go only because I hope you'll do a favor for me."

"And what would that be?"

Raith hesitated, but then folded his arms and looked at the ground. "Tell Sydran I'm sorry."

"Sydran?" Reitrin remembered the name. Sydran was a member of the Secret Police. He was someone Clyde didn't like to work with. That was all she remembered.

"It's a long story," said Raith. "He and I are from the same story. It's my fault we were separated. Fevros is using blackmail to keep me here. So, I suggest you go before someone that's actually loyal to Fevros shows up."

Reitrin stared at the boy. She stepped back and Raith turned away and resumed his position on the other side of the table.

"Thank you," Reitrin said quietly. "I'll be sure to tell him." She left the kitchen.

Around the corner, Traitor stood with an arrow ready and Etakai was leaning against the wall, holding his chest and panting.

"Here." Reitrin knelt beside Etakai and handed him the water and then rummaged in her pocket for his pills.

"Chatty human," Traitor grumbled. "You're lucky Raith is so kind."

"You could hear us?" Reitrin whispered.

Traitor nodded.

"How much further to where Wyvetta is?" Reitrin asked as she helped Etakai take the pill. He was so shaky he could hardly hold the glass without it spilling.

"In the catacombs of the cathedral," Traitor explained. "We'll have to double back to get there. It's not too far."

"You brought us here to get the water for Etakai," Reitrin realized.

"As I said, you're lucky Raith was on guard in there. He and I are in a similar situation, only his cannot be sorted as easily."

The sound of approaching footsteps made Reitrin's heart jump. Someone was coming around the corner.

"It's the Warlock." Raith appeared in the doorway, waving Reitrin into the kitchen. "Hide in here. Quick."

Reitrin took Etakai and helped him into the kitchen. The two of them sat behind the door out of sight.

Raith and Traitor stood in the hallway.

"Little out of your jurisdiction, aren't you?" The man who approached them had shaggy brown hair, red eyes, and was dressed in black clothes with a long, worn-out jacket over top. He had a menacing aura that Reitrin could feel looming above her from inside the kitchen.

"What do you mean?" Raith asked. "I'm always

here."

"Ah," muttered the man. He had a tired look in his eyes as he stopped and gazed into the kitchen.

"There's no alcohol in there," said Traitor.

The man cast Traitor a cold look. "I can get my own whenever I want. What are you doing here? I thought you were supposed to be trailing that girl Fevros doesn't shut up about."

"I was relieved of my post," Traitor replied. "Not that it's any of your business, Luke."

"Lukivoien," the man shot. "Not even Fevros should call me Luke, but he seems to think we're friends."

"Aren't you?"

Lukivoien walked past them without an answer. He paused on the other side of the kitchen doorway and looked back at them. "Are you two up to something?"

"Are you?" Traitor replied. "Since when do you go anywhere without Fevros?"

"Fevros left me in charge for a while," Lukivoien replied. "It wasn't my idea. This place is boring. I want to go back to my own story, but Fevros is the one calling the shots so I'm stuck here until further notice." He walked away with his hands in his pockets. "Now is a good time to cause problems."

His footsteps faded and Reitrin moved to stand, but Etakai caught her arm and pulled her back down beside him.

"Wait," he breathed in her ear.

Reitrin's heart jumped. She glanced up at Etakai. His eyes looked clearer as he watched the door.

They heard another door close in the distance and

the menacing presence of Lukivoien vanished. Etakai released Reitrin's arm.

"He's gone," said Raith, entering the kitchen.

"He knew we were here," said Etakai.

"I think so too," said Raith. "No one knows that guy's story, but Fevros acts like they're best friends. We can't be sure if Lukivoien is really his friend or is being used like the rest of us."

Reitrin stood up and went to the hallway where Traitor was waiting.

"Fevros may not be away," Traitor told her. "Lukivoien is a warlock who has been helping the Eysheus. It is Lukivoien's magic making the shield around this cathedral. He knew we were here before we passed through the doors, so him acting calm is unnerving. We can't trust him."

"I didn't plan on trusting him," said Reitrin. "He has a frightening aura."

Etakai stood up, holding his hand over his chest. "We need to hurry. What's the fastest way to the catacombs?"

Chapter Seventeen
The Catacombs

The fastest route to the catacombs was down the garbage chute. Raith explained that it led to the basement level where a dumpster caught the garbage. From there, the dumpster was wheeled out to a ramp that led to a garage facing the street.

Reitrin shuddered. It stank of rotting food and mold. Discolored leftovers stuck to the metal slide of the shoot. It was large enough for a full-grown man to fit inside.

"It reeks," said Reitrin.

"When you land in the dumpster your scent will be disguised by it," Raith told her. "There are hounds guarding the catacombs from the inside."

"Where do we go once we reach the basement?" Etakai asked.

"There is a barred gate that guards a stone door," Raith explained. "There's a cross on it. You can't miss it. It's the only thing down there besides the ramp and dumpster. Once you open the gate an alarm will sound. Also, you won't be able to open the stone door from the inside if it shuts."

"Then how the hell do we get Wyvetta out?" Etakai growled.

"I will guard the door," Traitor said. "I can make sure it doesn't shut."

Etakai straightened up and looked at Reitrin. "I don't like this. It sounds like we're walking into an elaborate trap."

"It wouldn't be a first for us," said Reitrin.

"Someone is coming," said Traitor.

"Get going," said Raith, hurrying to the door to stall the person.

Reitrin grabbed a cloth from the counter and wrapped it around her face to muffle the rancid stench of the garbage shoot.

"See you down there," she said to Etakai and Traitor. She had to step up on a chair to reach the shoot.

The drop was sudden and went straight down. Reitrin's stomach jumped, then the tunnel cut off into open air. Reitrin crashed into the dumpster, landing on a pile of black bags.

Her knee exploded with pain. Reitrin cursed and rolled away from where she had landed. She didn't want Etakai to land on her when he came through. When she tried to stand her knee gave out and she fell back into the trash. She heard someone coming down the chute.

Etakai fell from the chute and crashed into the dumpster.

He wheezed in pain, holding his chest and cursing the universe. With a grunt he pushed himself up and moved out of the way just as Traitor fell out of the shoot.

"Are you both okay?" Traitor whispered. The fall had not fazed him.

"I hurt my knee when I fell." Reitrin could feel it throbbing.

"Good job," said Etakai as he crawled to her and took her knee. Reitrin winced as he prodded the joint to find what was wrong. "It's a sprain. If we wrap it up you'll be okay."

Reitrin nodded and untied the cloth from her face, passing it to him.

"This too," said Traitor, passing him a length of cloth with old bloodstains.

Etakai didn't ask why Traitor had it. He wrapped Reitrin's leg while Traitor kept watch. Reitrin was embarrassed to have become a nuisance, but Etakai was not scolding her.

"How is that?" he asked, tying a tight knot.

Reitrin put pressure on her leg. All she felt was a weak pain beneath the compact wrap. "Better."

"Then let's go." Etakai stood and climbed out of the dumpster. Reitrin followed him. Etakai helped her out while Traitor leapt over the side and landed silent as a breath on the stone floor.

The room was huge and stretched in all directions. There were thick pillars of stone supporting the ceiling. It was dark except for pockets of light from the street that peeked in from the narrow windows at the top of the walls. Reitrin saw car headlights passing by the short windows.

"We aren't that far underground," she muttered. She saw the ramp for the dumpster. It was steep and led to the top floor. Reitrin crouched down to look further up the ramp. There was a garage door at the top with blacked out windows.

"There's the gate." Traitor pointed in the other direction.

The gate was covered in cobwebs. Skid marks in the dust outside of it showed the door had recently been opened.

"So when we open the gate an alarm sounds,"

said Etakai. "And we can't shut the stone door or we'll be trapped. There are hounds on guard inside the catacombs so someone who can fight should go in. What is the plan exactly?" He looked at Traitor.

"I'll go in by myself," Reitrin said.

Etakai gawked at her. "You just sprained your knee. And you're not much of a fighter."

"Someone has to keep the door open," Reitrin told Etakai. "That's Traitor. When the alarm sounds there will be guards so someone has to hold them off without killing anyone. Only you can do that with your blue shield. So that leaves me–"

"To face the hounds, and find Wyvetta," Etakai retorted. "You'll get killed."

"Stop arguing," Traitor hissed. "It may be quiet down here, but raised voices can still be heard in the rooms above."

Etakai cursed and lowered his voice. "Fine." He scowled at Reitrin. "But what's your plan?"

"I'm going to have to play it by ear since I don't know what the layout is inside the catacombs," she explained. "Like you said, I'm not a fighter, so I probably can't kill the hounds."

"Fire can be useful," said Traitor. "There should be torches inside. Grab one as soon as you can. Light it when you need it."

Etakai scowled at him. "How is she going to do that? Magic?"

"No." Traitor reached inside his cloak and withdrew a flint and striking stone. He handed them to Reitrin. "Keep these close. There are a lot of things that can burn in the catacombs, including the dead bodies. Be careful where you start the fire."

"Thank you," said Reitrin as she pocketed the flint and stone.

"Okay, let's get this over with," said Etakai, marching to the gate.

The three of them stood before the large gate. It was so tall it reached the ceiling. The stone door behind it was not as tall. It was sunk into the stone wall behind the gate. There were praying angels carved into the wall on the inside.

Traitor stepped to the gate, turned the latch, and pulled it open.

Panic shot through the whole room.

The alarm was silent, sending a warning through the air in a way Reitrin had never felt before. Her heart raced. Movement on the floors above echoed through the basement.

"Here they come," said Traitor.

Etakai and Reitrin passed him and went to the stone door. Etakai pushed on it. It rotated inward on huge hinges that creaked angrily in protest.

Reitrin stepped inside.

Etakai caught her arm and pulled her into a hug. "Please be careful in there," he whispered.

Reitrin was startled. "I will," she promised. She returned the hug before pushing away and entering the darkness.

The tunnel sloped down and Reitrin searched the walls for one of the torches Traitor had mentioned. She spotted one ahead of her and seized it from the wall. The depth of darkness ahead of her made it difficult to resist lighting the torch then and there.

Behind her, Etakai's blue shield appeared. Reitrin glanced back then hurried into the darkness.

She couldn't waste time. Etakai was too weak to hold out much longer. At first her steps were confident, but then she slowed down. She couldn't see a thing.

There was a damp smell in the air and in the distance a dripping sound echoed every few seconds. Reitrin held her breath and used the torch to feel the walls. The torch was sticky with webs under her hand and she swatted away what felt like a spider on her fingers.

A huffing sound stopped Reitrin in her tracks. She felt for the wall and moved as close to it as she could. She held her breath and prayed the sound would fade.

The hound's panting and its claws tapping on the floor grew louder as it walked nearer. It was so close Reitrin could feel the warmth of the body near her legs. It snorted, turned, and headed back the way it had come.

An explosion from up the tunnel made the hound stop. It barked, making Reitrin jump. She heard its paws pattering as it raced up the tunnel to investigate the sound.

Reitrin hoped Etakai would be able to deal with the hound as well as whatever was happening at the gate.

She continued down into the catacombs.

Up ahead, she saw pale light. It illuminated the end of the tunnel and Reitrin saw the next room had four tall stone tombs.

Reitrin stepped into the room. She looked up. The dim light came through grates in the cathedral floor. She could see the dark ceiling of the room above. Reitrin heard footsteps pacing on the tiles overhead.

She passed through the open room, looking at the walls where there were small dusty doors marking more tombs. They were cast in shadows from the grate and Reitrin shivered. She hurried to the next tunnel and saw the next room had a gate in front of it. Reitrin approached the gate, then froze.

Two hounds were patrolling the inside of the room. She had not seen the first one, but these two were in faint light. Reitrin could have counted their ribs. Their heads were large with floppy ears and their tongues rolled out between their long teeth. It looked as if they had not eaten in weeks.

Reitrin held her breath and listened to their claws tapping the floor. She looked past them. There was another gate across the room. Through the gate, Reitrin saw the shadowy form of a girl lying in the shadows. Her hair was long, tangled, and she was watching the dogs with hollow eyes. The coat she wore was ragged, long, and had stained fur sewn along the collar and hem.

It had to be Wyvetta.

An explosion up the tunnel shook the catacombs and stones rattled loose from the ceiling. Reitrin looked at the hounds and then up the way she had come. There was no time to waste.

She dug the flint and stone from her pocket and held the torch between her knees. She struck the flint hard, but the first try smashed her thumb.

"Ouch." She licked the blood off her thumb and tried again as the hounds reacted to her cry. They jumped over each other, trying to get through the bars. Their howls were of desperate hunger.

Sparks caught on the torch. The webs and dust flared up on the oily cloth and Reitrin held up the torch. The orange light made the hound's eyes glow.

Fear gripped her, but she had to save Wyvetta. Traitor and Etakai were depending on her.

Chapter Eighteen
Fires of Hell

Reitrin went to the gate. The hounds were drooling and barking. They snapped at each other, fighting over which one would get to bite into Reitrin first.

"Get back," said Reitrin, fanning the flame at them. It burned the nose of one hound, which yelped and jumped back.

Reitrin lifted the latch of the gate. The hounds hunched down, ready to strike.

Before the gate opened the hounds ran at it. They slammed against the gate, pushing it open and throwing Reitrin back.

"No!" Wyvetta screamed from her prison.

Reitrin held the fire between her and the hounds. They snapped and circled, trying to get on either side of her. Reitrin backed towards the gate, then raced inside and slammed it shut behind her.

The hounds howled and barked angrily. The latch fell shut, locking them out.

Reitrin breathed in relief. She turned to the cage where Wyvetta knelt, staring at her.

"You're crazy," whispered the girl. She must have been around Reitrin's age. She was pale, filthy, and her hands were stitched up from many terrible cuts. "What are you doing here? Who are you?"

"Reitrin," she replied, going to the gate. "Traitor begged us to help save you."

"Traitor?" Wyvetta blushed when she whispered

his name. "But I … I was told he had abandoned me."

"Far from it," replied Reitrin. "He's waiting for you with my friend. We're going to have to move fast. There's no telling what's waiting for us up there." She opened the gate and Wyvetta ran out of the cage.

"Then we need to hurry," she said. "I must see this for myself."

"We have to get past them first," said Reitrin, looking at the hounds.

"Trap them back in here," Wyvetta suggested. "I saw how you did it. We'll do it again."

"That was a mistake that worked to my advantage," Reitrin admitted. "The door only swings that way so it will be hard to repeat." She went to the gate. The hounds backed up, watching her. Reitrin handed the torch to Wyvetta.

The hounds did not charge as Reitrin pushed open the gate and Wyvetta held the torch in front of her. They waited, but the hounds were not running at them. Reitrin led the way slowly out of the cage.

One hound pounced at Reitrin, but Wyvetta stepped in and shoved the fire in the hound's face. It howled with pain and raced back down the tunnel, shaking the embers from its eyes.

The ceiling shook as a rumble went through the cathedral.

"Is that a battle?" Wyvetta asked in alarm.

"Probably." Reitrin took the torch and Wyvetta's arm. She ran at the hounds. The one with the burned face ran, but the other dodged Reitrin and sank its fangs into her arm.

Reitrin cried out.

Wyvetta took the torch and nailed the hound in the eye.

It screamed and released Reitrin's arm.

"Run!" Reitrin shouted.

Wyvetta led the way back through the catacombs. Despite their burns, the hounds chased after them. Reitrin ran harder, hugging her bleeding arm, her lame knee forgotten. They passed the room of tombs and entered the next tunnel.

The hounds were at their heels. Wyvetta waved the flame behind them, making the hounds jerk back.

Ahead of them came the sound of clashing steel and shouting. Reitrin ran harder. She thought of Etakai and how weak he was. If he had dropped his shield his life would be in danger. They came closer to the exit. There was no blue shield. All Reitrin could see were red flames holding the stone door open.

She gasped. "What happened?"

The hounds nipped at her heels. Reitrin turned and kicked one in the jaw. It jerked away and the other jumped at Reitrin, but Wyvetta lashed out with the flame.

It was then the flame came to life. It snaked off the torch and slithered around the hounds. The hounds yelped and cried, jumping away from the fire.

Wyvetta dropped the torch. "How is it doing that?"

Reitrin stared at the flames, then turned and looked up the tunnel.

They weren't alone anymore. The familiar redhead stood at the top of the tunnel. There was soot on his face and embers on the sleeves of his black blouse. His black eyes had a red glow.

"Aoiro?" Reitrin demanded.

"Hurry," he snapped. "I have to get you two out of here before more enemies come."

Reitrin and Wyvetta raced up the tunnel as the flames distracted the hounds. As they reached the exit, the red fire climbed the walls around them. Aoiro was frighteningly powerful. He led them into the tunnel of red fire.

They reached the giant gate. Outside there was a wall of red fire passing through the center of the stone basement to guide them to the open garage.

"Get out of here," Aoiro called, stopping outside the gate and waving the girls forward. "Follow that path and don't stop. The Secret Police are waiting outside."

Wyvetta ran ahead, but Reitrin hesitated beside Aoiro. "Where are Etakai and Traitor?"

"Traitor is safe," said Aoiro quickly. "Etakai is in bad shape. He's in custody of the Secret Police now."

"What happened?"

"Go!" Aoiro shoved her towards the exit. "Why do women talk so much?"

Reitrin glared at him, but just then the roar of the flames grew louder. Aoiro looked up and cursed. The red of the fire was turning light blue at the top.

"Fevros." Aoiro seized Reitrin and ran up the path with her. Ahead of them Wyvetta made it outside. As soon as she was through, a wall of blue fire shot up in front of the ramp.

Aoiro stopped, pulling Reitrin back with him. The red fire swirled purple and then died down to blue embers on the ground. A chill swept through the room.

Fevros stood across from them

"My, my," muttered Fevros, looking around the room. There were bloodstains, burn marks, lost weapons, and unconscious warriors. "What damage was caused while I was away? Incredible." He looked up, his blue eyes blazing with rage, but he smiled.

"And you," Fevros continued, walking forward. "Aoiro, my old friend, what brings you here?"

"Stopping fools from destroying storybooks by killing your guards," Aoiro replied.

Reitrin heard the fear in Aoiro's voice.

"And I see you have that irritating girl," said Fevros. He stopped before them, looking from one to the other.

"The only one I could catch," Aoiro explained. His grip on Reitrin's arm tightened.

"Interesting." Fevros's smile widened and then he laughed. "My old friend, do you think I'm a fool? You may try your hardest to trick me, but I know who this girl is."

Aoiro gave a start, but then the red of his eyes flared to life. He shoved Reitrin down and lifted his hands as Fevros's lightning blue eyes gleamed.

Blue and red fire exploded from the ground around them.

Reitrin screamed and covered her head.

The flames roared, blazing back and forth like snakes, crashing through pillars, slamming into each other and exploding with each strike. Wherever they passed, they left burn marks in the stone. Aoiro stood over Reitrin. His hands snapped back and forth, conducting the red fire to deflect the blue flames of

Fevros

Reitrin peeked over her arms, past Aoiro's ankles, to Fevros who used one hand to control his fire and wore a bored expression. When Reitrin looked at Aoiro's face, the man was grimacing and the red fire singed his fingertips.

An upward slice of Aoiro's hand and the red fire cut through the blue and shot at Fevros. The man sidestepped with ease. He took a pipe from inside his coat, held it out to the flames to light it, and then bit down on it with an evil smile.

"You can't play halfhearted with me, Aoiro," Fevros shouted. His blue flames rushed around him like a typhoon. "Why not kill me?" He laughed maniacally as if he had made a great joke.

"Reitrin," Aoiro whispered.

Reitrin looked up at him. She was alarmed to see blood drip from his eye.

"Run to the exit. I'll hold him off. Tell Hiro that Fevros knows my secret." Aoiro looked down at her, the blood sliding down his face like tears. "Please."

Chills of fear swept over Reitrin. She nodded and stood up. "Will you be okay?"

"It doesn't matter," Aoiro hissed. "Get out of here before I end up getting myself killed to protect you."

Reitrin clenched her jaw and ran for the exit.

"Hey!" Fevros roared. The blue flames shot at Reitrin. They exploded like a firework and cut her off.

Reitrin skidded to a stop, but then red fire flew past her. It exploded into the blue flames and cut a trail to the exit. Reitrin ran up the ramp, but at the top she paused to look back.

Aoiro was staring at her. He was pale and the blood from his eyes dripped off his frightened face. Reitrin held his gaze.

Blue fire slammed into Aoiro. He crashed to the ground and did not move.

"No!" Reitrin cried. She ran back and knelt to roll him over. There were burns on his face and clothes and the blood from his eyes was smeared on his cheeks.

"Wake up," Reitrin said, shaking him. "Wake up, Aoiro."

Fevros was laughing. "What a waste. The man sacrificed himself to save you and you come running right back into my grasp."

Reitrin yelled when Fevros grabbed the back of her neck and pulled her to her feet. His fingers were cold and his grip like iron. Tears sprang into Reitrin's eyes.

"I could finish you right now if I wanted to, but I want Aoiro to be awake to see it."

"Put her down."

Fevros whipped around. He released Reitrin who crashed to her knees. She cringed and looked up.

It was Hiro, but not the Hiro Reitrin knew. He strode forward in full armor made of shining gold and silver. A mask was closed over his mouth and nose. The helmet came to a point above his eyes and his black hair was straight back and jagged. The top of the helmet appeared to have two pointed ears at the top.

Fevros's jaw dropped. "Oh, you're–"

Hiro punched Fevros in the face.

Fevros flew across the room. He slammed into the far wall and the stone crumbled around him. He lifted his head, his blue eyes gleaming with rage.

"I don't like interfering with your dispute," Hiro said. His voice echoed and there was a luminous shine behind his golden eyes as if his body were full of light. "But this chaos has drawn too much attention."

"Back off, Goldy," Fevros growled. He pulled himself free from the wall and shook the stones off his coat. "They're trespassing on my land. I can do as I want with them."

"Let's not argue over laws," Hiro said. He picked up Aoiro and hoisted him over his shoulder. "We both know how this ends, do we not?"

Fevros spat blood from his mouth. "Golden scum. You're just lucky I wasted my energy playing with that weak excuse for an Eysheus."

"It is strategy, not luck." Hiro turned away, then grabbed Reitrin and tossed her over his other shoulder. Reitrin was startled and Hiro's armor poked her ribs. She stared back at Fevros as Hiro carried her and Aoiro to the exit.

Fevros was watching her. A twisted smile spread across his face and he waved.

"See you again," he called.

Reitrin's blood ran cold with terror.

Chapter Nineteen
The Other Story

Etakai watched Reitrin as she ran down the tunnel into the catacombs. He hoped she would be okay. There was no telling what would be waiting for her in the darkness.

Traitor shut the gate. "They're coming. And this gate won't keep their weapons out."

"I know," said Etakai, turning away from the tunnel. "I can handle it." He was still weak and dizzy. The medicine had dulled the pain, but it could not replace the energy he lacked. He would only use the shield when it was necessary.

The clamor of feet charged into the basement from different angles. Archers lined up, drew their arrows, and fired.

Etakai lifted his hand. His blue eye blazed and the shield went up. The arrows stuck in the shield then sank to the ground as if it were jelly.

"Your shield seems weak," Traitor commented.

"It is," Etakai growled. "I have to focus. Can you hold the door open? I can't do both."

Traitor ran past Etakai and braced the door with his foot and shoulder. He had his bow and arrows ready, but since they couldn't kill the attackers without destroying their stories, he was not anxious to use them.

The enemy's arrows kept coming. One passed through the shield and clattered to the ground at Traitor's feet.

"This is bad," Etakai whispered. Sweat drizzled down his face and his blue eye ached. "I can't keep the shield up."

Traitor drew back his arrow. "I didn't want it to come to this. How much longer can you last?"

Etakai shook his head. His sight was blurring. He saw there were more people outside the gate. Knights, warriors, assassins—all of them dark people from the depths of the strangest stories. Characters like him. Plucked from their pages to play their part in a game the Eysheus started. None of them had a choice. Like Raith and Traitor, most of them were only there because they were blackmailed by Fevros.

Five threats ran at the shield and slammed into it.

Etakai jerked back and the blue shield weakened, but then one of the characters shouted.

"Move aside!"

The threats ran and a black shiny sphere flew at the weak shield. Etakai saw the lit fuse too late.

The bomb exploded and Etakai was thrown back against the stone door that creaked on its hinges.

Traitor shouted and Etakai heard him letting arrows fly. Threats screamed. Traitor shouted for Etakai to wake up and help him.

Etakai shook his head, then heard a howl coming from the catacombs. He whipped around when a gangly hound with yellow eyes ran at him from the tunnel behind them. Its drooling fangs snapped at Etakai, who dodged at the last moment and kicked the dog in the ribs. It yelped and ran at him again.

"Damn it all," Traitor barked, firing more arrows. "Not killing them is a hassle."

Etakai drew a knife and summoned as much

energy as he could muster to slam it down into the hound's neck. The hound died and Etakai crashed to his knees, panting.

The stone door began to shut. Traitor jumped back in its path and braced it open, firing more arrows.

"I'm running out of arrows," he yelled.

Etakai looked out at the characters that were falling back, holding the arrows in their shoulders or knees.

Traitor was hitting them in painful spots, but not fatal. The arrows the enemy had fired at them were laying beyond their reach. If Traitor could reach them he would have plenty.

Etakai wished he had more strength, but he could not wait around for it any longer.

"I'm going into the fray," he said.

"I'll cover you," Traitor promised.

Etakai ran out of the gate into the basement. Three characters met him; one cloaked and wielding a short sword, another was a knight in black armor with a broadsword, and one wearing furs and leather and wielding two Bowie knives.

They attacked Etakai who avoided the cloaked man's sword, blocked the knight's attack with his arm, and broke the nose of the man in the furs. He ducked under the cloaked man's second strike and kicked the weapon out of the man's hand. As the knight swung at him, Etakai jumped in the air. The sword whipped past him, cutting the cloaked man's arm.

Blood splattered to the ground. Etakai slammed his feet on the knight's shoulders, crashing to the ground with him. The cloaked man fell back, and two more opponents ran in to face Etakai. One got an arrow in his shin from Traitor and hit the ground screaming.

Etakai could hardly see as he blocked the fists flying at him. One caught him in the jaw. He crashed to the ground, but scrambled to his feet.

The garage door exploded.

Etakai and the enemies stared at it as red fire engulfed the exit. It rolled along the ceiling and floor. Characters and creatures near it raced away.

Etakai gritted his teeth. Aoiro.

The Eysheus strode down the ramp. His black eyes glowed red. He lifted his hands and the flames shot towards Etakai.

Etakai cringed, but the fire didn't touch him. It cut between him and the man he had been fighting, then turned and shot to the gate where Traitor stood. The flames reached the ceiling, creating a barrier between them and the enemies.

"Where's Reitrin?" Aoiro demanded as he strode down the path he'd created. "What the hell do you think you're doing endangering her?"

"She's in the catacombs fetching Wyvetta," Traitor replied. "It was she who led this mission, not Etakai."

Aoiro flicked his hand. A stream of fire grabbed the stone door beside Traitor and forced it open.

"Out!" Aoiro roared. "Both of you."

Traitor wasted no time fleeing the basement.

Etakai staggered away from Aoiro, but fell to the ground. When he tried to stand, his head swam and his sight went dark.

"Seriously?" Aoiro grumbled. "Glen! Get this dying idiot out of here."

Etakai heard this but he could see nothing. Someone picked him up. He was carried out of the basement into the cool of night.

"Chief, are you sure Lukivoien lowered the shield?" Glen whispered from somewhere outside Etakai's foggy mind.

"We will have to investigate his background," Hiro replied. He was near them, possibly walking with them, Etakai wasn't sure. "As my right-hand man, I'll leave that task up to you. He may just be one who likes to cause trouble."

"Gee, thanks. What did he hope to gain from this then?"

"We cannot be sure. Take that one to headquarters. He needs serious medical attention."

Etakai felt himself placed in the back of a vehicle. Someone strapped his arms down. It was a necessary precaution. The last time he blacked out, his unconscious body had attacked everyone with his green fire, nearly killing them.

The engine rumbled and the car drove away. From the front seat Etakai still heard voices. They were talking about Aoiro, saying he was acting strange and should not have gone into the cathedral.

Etakai's mind spun. Reitrin had been right about Aoiro. He didn't know what to believe. For now, he could only hope Reitrin would escape safely.

Chapter Twenty
Sacrifice of a Hero

Reitrin sat in the back seat of Hiro's too-familiar sedan. Now she could understand why it had a lingering scent of blood. This couldn't have been the first time there was a wounded person in the car.

This time the person was Aoiro.

He lay on the seat beside Reitrin. She had a towel on her leg where his head was resting. The blood from his eyes rolled down his face without showing signs of stopping.

Reitrin had questions, but she didn't dare speak. Hiro was furious and it was frightening.

As soon as she and Aoiro were in the car, Hiro's golden armor sank into his body. He wore his plain black uniform beneath the armor. Reitrin knew she would never understand how Hiro's abilities worked. His armor was a part of him, but materializing it kept his skin and clothes intact.

He drove them down the dark road, taking a roundabout way to their headquarters. He was speaking in code into his phone as he drove. None of what he said made sense to Reitrin, but she guessed he was making sure no one was following them.

When he fell silent Reitrin dared to speak.

"Why are his eyes bleeding?" Her voice sounded small when it broke the heavy silence.

"Do you need to ask that?" Hiro glanced at Reitrin through the rear-view mirror. "Can't you guess?"

Reitrin bit her lip. "He used too much power to save me."

"Bingo." Hiro shook his head. "What were you thinking? How could you lead Etakai and Traitor into the heart of Fevros's domain?"

"I just wanted to help Traitor," Reitrin whispered. Tears welled up in her eyes. "I didn't realize what that place was at first. I'm sorry, Hiro. I didn't want anyone to get hurt."

"But that's what happens," said Hiro. "When you try to be the hero you get hurt. Look at Etakai. Look at Aoiro. Look at yourself."

Reitrin gazed at the dog bite on her arm. It pulsed beneath the cloth Hiro had given her to wrap it with. Her blood soaked the cloth and she clenched her jaw.

"Now you know what happens to heroes in the Real World," Hiro said. "How do you feel?"

Reitrin wiped the tears from her eyes. "Terrible."

"Really?" Hiro glanced at her again. "Wyvetta is safe with Traitor at headquarters. You accomplished your mission, but Etakai and Aoiro are unconscious because of it."

"What are you trying to prove?" Reitrin whispered. "That I'm not good enough?"

"No. I want you to realize this isn't a game. You've been dealt a tough hand in life. I hope you're strong enough to handle what comes with it."

Reitrin stared at him, then gazed at Aoiro. "Hiro … I was supposed to tell you that Fevros knows Aoiro's secret."

Hiro was silent. Reitrin looked at him and saw his expression was dark.

"I see," he said at last.

"What does that mean?"

"It's not good for you," Hiro replied. He came to a curve in the road and hit a button on his visor. Reitrin watched as the ground at the corner lifted, revealing a hidden passage.

"You have entrances all over the place," Reitrin commented as Hiro drove into the darkness.

"We can't risk being trapped," Hiro replied.

They were silent as Hiro drove down the passage. It swept around and went on in a wide circle for a long time. Finally, the tunnel widened and they pulled up to a familiar gate with two guards.

"Hiro," said a man with long red hair. "Is Aoiro with you? Etakai and the others are inside but we–"

"I have him, Sydran." Hiro nodded over his shoulder. The man leaned in and Reitrin recognized him. The long red hair and black lips were impossible to forget. She had met this man before, when the Secret Police had first shown up.

"You're Sydran, right?" she asked quickly.

"Yes," he said, giving her a surprised look. He looked at Aoiro and cringed at his condition. "I've never seen him like this." He turned away and waved to the second guard, who pulled the lever to open the gate.

"Sydran!" Reitrin called before Hiro could move the car. "Do you know a boy named Raith?"

Sydran practically jumped into the car through Hiro's window.

"Raith?" Sydran's blue eyes were wide with alarm. "You know him? You met him? Is he okay?"

The terror on his face broke Reitrin's heart. "Yes, I met him. He's working for Fevros. He wanted me to tell you he's sorry."

Sydran stared at her as if he could not believe his ears. "He's working for Fevros?"

"He said Fevros is using blackmail to keep him there," Reitrin explained. "Like how he was using Wyvetta to control Traitor."

Sydran narrowed his eyes, but pulled himself out of the car and gazed at Hiro, who was frowning.

"I didn't hear about that until now," Hiro told him. "I'm sorry."

"At least we know he's not dead," Sydran whispered. His voice was hoarse.

Hiro frowned. "How long is it until you're relieved of your post?"

"A few hours."

"I'll send someone to replace you before then," said Hiro. "And if we can, we'll have someone sniff out what Fevros is using as blackmail. I can't guarantee we'll find anything, but we can try."

"Thank you." Sydran stepped back from the car.

Reitrin watched him as Hiro drove through the open gate. Sydran was fighting back tears.

"When can I see Etakai?" Reitrin asked.

"After you and I have a chance to speak of what transpired tonight," Hiro replied. He pulled into a parking spot. As soon as he turned off the car the doors of the hideout opened and three men in white lab coats ran out with a stretcher.

Reitrin was caught in the chaos of the men taking Aoiro out of the car and setting him on the stretcher. When they moved him, Reitrin thought she saw his eyes open slightly to look at her.

The doctors took him away before Reitrin could

even get out of the car. Hiro closed his door and went to Reitrin's. He looked down at her and she met his gaze. Tears rolled down her face.

"Let's get our meeting over with," he said, nodding to the door. "I have tissues in my office."

Reitrin swallowed hard and nodded. She got out of the car and Hiro shut the door. The pain in her knee had returned. She walked with a slight limp because of it.

Hiro led Reitrin up the stairs and into the busy hallway. No one bothered Hiro this time. They soon reached the control room with all the monitors. People were shouting and talking on phones more than the last time. Chaos filled the air and Reitrin shivered.

"Send a replacement guard to relieve Sydran at the third gate," Hiro called into the room. One man in black jumped up, saluted, and then left the room through a sliding glass door.

Hiro led Reitrin down the stairs to his office. He opened the door and let Reitrin in.

As soon as she entered the room the dinging sound went off over her head. She frowned up at it.

Hiro shut the door and snapped his fingers. "Private meeting," he told the door. "But I'm expecting guests. Summon Belle too."

The door chimed its understanding.

Hiro pulled back a chair for Reitrin then went behind the desk. He searched the drawers and returned with a box of tissues.

"Okay," said Hiro. He did not sit behind his desk. He took the seat beside Reitrin's and turned it to face her. He offered her the tissues which she accepted gratefully as she sank into her seat.

"What do you need to know?" Reitrin whispered into the tissues.

"How you like your tea," replied Hiro, setting the box aside.

Reitrin gave him a puzzled look. "What are you talking about?" She sniffed and wiped her nose on the tissue. "What does tea have to do with this?"

"Everything," replied Hiro. "Do you want coffee instead?"

Reitrin shook her head.

There came a knock on the door.

"Enter," Hiro called.

A woman slipped inside, shutting the door behind her. She wore a black dress with a white jacket. Her eyes were clear blue and her short hair was an array of black, white, brown, and tan. She tilted her head, giving Hiro a curious look.

"Good timing, Belle," said Hiro.

"What do you need?" Belle asked. Her voice was nasally. It almost made her sound like a cat.

"A pot of chamomile tea," replied Hiro. "Bring sugar and milk. I also will need you to check her arm. Dog bite."

"Understood," said Belle. She slipped back out of the room. The door shut behind her and Hiro turned back to Reitrin.

"Are you feeling alright?"

Reitrin gave him a confused look. "Why are you being nice?"

Hiro heaved a sigh. "The events of this day could be traumatizing for you. It may not have dawned upon you, but I've seen it happen many times. You played hero twice and endangered a dear friend of mine. But besides that, you also endangered your own friend."

Reitrin felt the tears fill her eyes again when she thought of Etakai lying somewhere in pain.

"I'm so stupid," she sobbed into the tissues. "He wouldn't let me go alone, but I shouldn't have even gone. He almost died last week and now he's in worse condition than before."

Hiro listened to her weep. She tried to speak more, but none of it was audible because of her hiccups and the tissue in her face. When her sobbing died down Hiro sighed.

"And this is why the tea matters."

Reitrin glanced at him with swollen eyes.

Hiro smiled sadly. "Being the one who saves people also means you're the one who loses people. I have suffered great loss to become what I am today. Aoiro and Etakai are the same. Loss is a part of this, Ms. Nichol. You did not lose anyone today. There were injuries, but no casualties. You got off easy."

Reitrin bowed her head.

Belle returned with a tray of tea. She placed it on the desk without a word then went to Reitrin. As she unwrapped the cloth on Reitrin's arm, Hiro poured the tea.

Belle cleaned the bite mark, examining it before applying salve and wrapping it up. "It's surprisingly mild. You won't need stitches."

"Surprising indeed," said Hiro. He passed a cup of tea to Reitrin. "Thank you, Belle."

Belle nodded and left the office.

Reitrin glanced at the bandages on her arm, then

reached for the sugar and milk.

"I'll remember you take both," said Hiro as he drank his tea plain. "So next time I won't have to ask and waste precious therapy time."

Reitrin gazed at Hiro. She couldn't understand him. "I thought you were mad."

"Oh, I am," replied Hiro. "I'm furious that you caused Aoiro to bring himself to the brink of death for no reason. You also broke an unspoken treaty. The Secret Police knew not to invade the cathedral or risk unleashing Fevros's wrath. We had no choice in this matter, but it will set things into motion that cannot be stopped."

Reitrin ducked her head.

"However, you accomplished your goal. You set Traitor free from Fevros and now he is safely in our care here with Wyvetta. He was a terrible enemy and now we have him as an ally. I thank you for that. Their story will survive and when Aoiro is healed, he can seal it so Fevros never gets in again."

"He can do that?" Reitrin whispered.

"Yes, but it takes a lot of energy, so he only uses the ability when it's necessary," explained Hiro.

The two of them drank tea in silence a while longer.

"What's going to happen to me now?" Reitrin asked, gazing into the teacup.

"That's yet to be seen," muttered Hiro. He rubbed his chin thoughtfully. "Aoiro's secret is something I cannot tell you, but you must know its discovery has put you and those you love in danger."

"Figures," muttered Reitrin.

"We will place more guards around you," Hiro

concluded. "You, your hotel, and that restaurant you will be working at."

"The Hideaway," said Reitrin with a nod.

"Yes. For the time being that is how we shall proceed. If more steps are needed for your protection we will do what we must."

"Can I ask you something?" Reitrin glanced at Hiro who raised an eyebrow at her.

"What is it?"

"Why didn't Fevros fight you?"

"Ah, that," Hiro muttered. "Yes, well, it's not too complicated. I was stronger than him today."

"Just today?"

"Fevros had been fighting with Aoiro," Hiro explained. "He may not have shown it, but he was tired, whereas I had full strength. He knew that messing with me would be a bad idea so he let me leave. I was lucky for that. I played it off as a strategy, but the truth of the matter is I didn't want to interfere. Fevros is Aoiro's enemy. I hoped the two of them meeting could solve the problem, but all it did was make things worse."

"Why couldn't you have come sooner?" Reitrin asked.

"Aoiro requested I wait for you outside and take you to safety," replied Hiro. "That was our plan. It was simple and should have worked, but then you didn't escape with Wyvetta like Aoiro hoped you would. If you had run when you had a chance, Aoiro would have made it out as well. The moment you stopped to look back at him, the plan failed. When you ran back to him, I had to compromise to save you both."

Reitrin ducked her head. "I'm sorry."

"What's done is done."

Reitrin hesitated. "Can I see Etakai now?"

Hiro finished his tea and nodded. "I'll bring you to him. Before that, you have to give me your report. My men saw you and Etakai leave the hotel with Traitor, but none of my men were sure when he slipped inside the hotel. I don't like that. They didn't sense menace, so they reported your movement and followed instead of intercepting you. I had Aoiro on standby, but for obvious reasons he cannot report what happened from his end."

"Traitor never left the hotel," Reitrin said. "He told us he had been hiding inside since before we were relocated there."

Hiro sat back with a frown. "I see." He was silent for a moment, but then sighed. "How about you tell me the rest of your report now?"

"Okay." Reitrin's heart sank. She didn't want to relive her stupid decision again, but she began her story, starting from the moment Aoiro dropped her off at the hotel.

Chapter Twenty-One
The Hospital Wing

With her report concluded, Reitrin followed Hiro down many different hallways, up an elevator, and into a quiet hall that was not as bright or as busy.

"Where are we now?" Reitrin whispered.

"Hospital wing," replied Hiro. "Etakai's room is up ahead."

"Can I see Aoiro too?"

"They're in the same room."

Reitrin thought that was a bad idea. When they woke, the hospital wing could be blown up.

Hiro brought her to a door with a thin window. Inside, the room was pale tan and had four beds. There were closed curtains around two of the beds, but the other two were empty.

Reitrin's heart was racing. The men she was about to visit were suffering because of her mistakes.

She followed Hiro through the door.

The nurse looked up from the bed at the far corner. She had brown hair wrapped up in two buns that looked like ears on top of her head. Her uniform was light blue with a white apron, and she wore gloves.

When she saw Hiro, she smiled. "Do you have another one for me to look at?"

"Dog bite," replied Hiro. "And a sprained knee. Belle already checked the bite. I'd like her to rest here with her friends as well after you've checked her out."

"Over here, young lady," said the nurse.

Reitrin followed her and the nurse had her sit on the empty bed.

"Are you hurt, Chief?" The nurse looked back at Hiro.

"No, I'm fine, Laufsy," Hiro replied. "I am sure you can tell, but I plan on keeping these three here for quite a while. Are you fine with that?"

"Yes, I understand," replied Laufsy.

"Me too?" Reitrin asked. "My injuries aren't that bad though."

"I want to keep an eye on you," Hiro answered. "So yes, you'll stay in headquarters for the time being."

"Oh." Reitrin wasn't sure if she liked that.

"I'm going back to my office," Hiro told Reitrin. "You'll only stay in this room temporarily. I'll take care of the arrangements to have you settled into a proper room later."

Hiro left and Laufsy went to Aoiro's bed, pushing open the curtains halfway. Reitrin peered past her.

Aoiro had bandages over his eyes and salve for the burns on his face. He was lying on his back and Reitrin saw his fingertips were also bandaged.

Seeing him made Reitrin's heart sink. She bit her lip and glanced at the other bed that was still closed off by its curtains. She was almost scared to know what injuries Etakai had suffered because of her.

"Can I visit my friend?" Reitrin asked.

"Of course," said Laufsy. "I'll be making my rounds now. If you need anything, ring the buzzer by your bed." She pointed to the white button on the wall behind the bed. With that, Laufsy left the room.

Reitrin stood up and crossed the room. She gazed at Aoiro for a few seconds before turning back to Etakai's bed.

"Etakai?" She called. "Are you awake?" When he didn't reply, she hesitated before pushing back the curtain to peek inside.

Etakai glared at her with only his green eye.

"A dog bite?" he inquired spitefully. "I drain all my energy and you leave with just a dog bite?"

"Should I have let it rip my whole arm off?" Reitrin demanded. "Would that make you feel better?"

Etakai snorted. "I have a headache, don't start yelling."

"I won't," Reitrin muttered. "If I wake Aoiro then the two of you will probably finish each other off."

Etakai shook his head and glanced towards Aoiro's bed. "I saw the nasty state he is in. What happened?"

"He used too much energy," Reitrin whispered. She sat on the edge of Etakai's bed, gazing at Aoiro. "Fevros showed up when we were leaving."

She told Etakai what had happened. It was the second time she had told the story, but shame was fresh in her voice. She looked at the ground with tears hanging in her eyes.

"It's hard to hate him after a story like that," Etakai said. "But I still don't trust him."

Reitrin gazed at Etakai sadly. She couldn't blame Etakai for his mistrust. Aoiro was the one who had removed him from his story.

"How are you feeling? Reitrin asked to change the subject.

"Weak," replied Etakai. "I'm probably about as weak as you are."

Reitrin glared at him. "Ouch. That was a cheap shot."

"It's all I've got right now, sorry." Etakai smirked at her. "Honestly, I can't believe we survived that mess in the cathedral. I thought for sure we would all die down there."

Reitrin gave him a puzzled look.

"What?" he asked.

"You and Aoiro are in terrible shape," Reitrin replied. "How can you be glad?"

Etakai shrugged. "We accomplished what we set out to do. None of us died. We came close, but I think Aoiro will pull through. That man is like a cockroach."

"Thanks," grumbled Aoiro.

Reitrin's heart leapt, and she went to his bedside. "Aoiro?"

"I'm tired," muttered Aoiro. "Leave me alone. Women," he heaved a sigh. "They don't shut up."

Reitrin gawked at him.

"Why does he keep saying that to me?" She turned to Etakai, but his eyes were shut as if he were asleep.

"You did not fall asleep that fast."

Etakai made his breathing deeper and Reitrin rolled her eyes.

"Whatever," she said, throwing her hands in the air. "At least you're both alive. I can rest peacefully." She strode to the empty bed and threw back the covers. As she kicked off her shoes, she heard Etakai chuckle.

"Sleep well," he said.

Reitrin heaved a long sigh and smiled in his direction. "You too. I'm glad you're both alive."

"She still isn't shutting up," Aoiro groaned.

"Will you quit that?" Reitrin snapped.

"Get some sleep, Rei," Etakai muttered tiredly. "I'm seconds away from agreeing with him."

"Fine, whatever," Reitrin shot back. She crawled into bed and pulled the covers up to her chin. Even though the day had been one of the worst ones of her life, Reitrin was smiling. She hugged the hospital pillow and felt herself drift into much-needed slumber.

To Be Continued

www.ingramcontent.com/pod-product-compliance
Lightning Source LLC
Chambersburg PA
CBHW021708190726

48289CB00008B/2432